"Let's go, then, before it gets dark."

Rose gave Oscar the command to stay back in order to give the man space and not upset him further.

The stranger slowly stood, leaning against the boulder for support. This guy wouldn't get very far if he could barely stand.

Adjusting his backpack, he took a few steps.

In the wrong direction.

"The trail is back this way," she said.

He turned to her. "They'll find me if I take the trail."

"Who?"

Without answering, he continued walking away from her and stumbled. Rose rushed to his side and gripped his arm to help him remain steady. When he glanced at her, Rose's breath caught at the look of defeat in his eyes.

"Hey, you're going to be okay," she said.

He pulled away and continued toward the dense forest. He wasn't thinking clearly, paranoid about someone out to get him.

"Please, sir, going that way isn't a good idea. Let me—"

A gunshot echoed through the forest.

The stranger dropped to the ground as Rose dove for cover.

An eternal optimist, **Hope White** was born and raised in the Midwest. She and her college sweetheart have been married for thirty years and are blessed with two wonderful sons, two feisty cats and a bossy border collie. When not dreaming up inspirational tales, Hope enjoys hiking, sipping tea with friends and going to the movies. She loves to hear from readers, who can contact her at hopewhiteauthor@gmail.com.

Visit the Author Profile page at LoveInspired.com.

TRACING
A FUGITIVE

HOPE WHITE

LOVE INSPIRED SUSPENSE
INSPIRATIONAL ROMANCE

LOVE INSPIRED® SUSPENSE
INSPIRATIONAL ROMANCE

Recycling programs for this product may not exist in your area.

ISBN-13: 978-1-335-72314-7

Tracing a Fugitive

Love Inspired
22 Adelaide St. West, 41st Floor
Toronto, Ontario M5H 4E3, Canada
www.LoveInspired.com

Printed in U.S.A.

For I was an hungred, and ye gave me meat: I was thirsty, and ye gave me drink: I was a stranger, and ye took me in.
—*Matthew* 25:35

This book is dedicated to US veterans,
who sacrifice so much in order to protect our freedoms.

ONE

Noah Greene stopped abruptly on the mountain trail.

Waited.

Listened.

Heard nothing but the usual sounds of nature: birds chirping, the wind whistling, water bubbling from a nearby creek.

Yet deep in his core he knew…

They'd found him.

How had they tracked him so quickly from two thousand miles away?

Noah increased his pace to a jog. Had to put distance between him and the men on the hunt.

He struggled to calm the adrenaline rush, his heart racing with the prospect of what might happen next. If he was caught, he knew they'd be brutal, tormenting him until he gave them the answer they wanted—the location of his best friend.

Which he would never do, even if he knew exactly where Thomas was, which he didn't.

Therefore, Noah would most likely die out here in the Montana mountains.

The same mountains where he'd hoped to find Thomas in a remote cabin away from the false accusations and threats to his life. Authorities suspected him of selling code to foreign agents to access US government servers.

Noah refused to believe his friend had betrayed his country. He knew Thomas better than that. As US soldiers, they had served together, nearly died together, fighting insurgents in Afghanistan. They had both risked their lives to protect their country. Thomas would not disrespect what they'd worked so hard to protect...for money.

Noah would never abandon Thomas, just as Thomas had not abandoned Noah on the battle-field.

Which made Noah a target running from the enemy, and no closer to finding his friend. He'd been so careful when he'd left Virginia, careful not to leave a trace of information about his final destination: Montana, Big Sky Country, where Thomas claimed one could fall off the grid, dis-appear in the wilderness.

As if you'd never existed.

Thomas described it as a refuge, a safe place.

Noah forged ahead, aiming for tall green pine trees that would provide cover from his enemies, who he assumed were foreign agents.

The crack of a gunshot made him drop to the ground. He sucked in a deep breath and struggled to push down the haunting memories of war.

"Not now," he ground out.

He couldn't let the trauma paralyze him, not

today, not if he wanted to survive. Scrambling to his feet, he headed up the trail away from the sound, hoping to block it out so he could focus on disappearing in the wilderness in order to stay alive.

At thirty-four he was too young to die. He had wrongs to right, redemption to earn, if that was even possible.

Another crack of gunfire made him duck, but he didn't go down this time. He wouldn't give up without a fight.

The sound of barking dogs triggered panic as a memory shot to the surface, being caught, corralled, attacked by a dog. His hands started shaking.

"Keep breathing," he coached himself.

The dogs would easily find him unless he did something to throw them off. He changed course and aimed for a mountain wall up ahead. The animals wouldn't be able to follow him and would lose his scent. It would buy him time to escape.

The story of his life, escaping, running. He thought the IT security job had finally offered a reprieve.

"Over there!" a man shouted.

Noah dived into nearby brush, pine needles scratching his cheeks. His focus locked on the rocky refuge ahead, he tried shutting down ghosts of the past.

He scrambled toward his destination. Nearly

there. He spotted a crevice up above on the rocky slope, a spot where he could hide until the threat passed. It looked wide enough for a man to take cover, but would they think to look up? Would he be too exposed?

He had no choice.

He jogged to the rocky slope and hoped the surrounding evergreens would camouflage his ascent. They wouldn't expect him to go off trail, into the wilderness.

Reaching the rock wall, he took a deep, steadying breath and started to climb.

Higher, higher. Pressing his cheek against the cool stone, he fought the violent memories clawing their way to the surface, memories that could trigger his post-traumatic stress.

"Breathe," he said and did his four-square breathing technique to calm himself.

He looked up and reached for another protruding rock. Placed his foot in a secure position and hoisted himself up. Took another deep breath.

You can do this. For Thomas.

He continued climbing and moved to the left, out of sight. A few minutes later he was nearing the ledge that could provide temporary safety. He glanced down, realizing this side of the mountain overlooked a steep drop. Anxiety knotted in his gut. He pushed it aside.

I'm coming, Thomas. I'll find you. I'll save you.

Like Thomas had saved Noah.

The sudden memory shot his concentration to pieces.

His foot slipped, but he held on with determined fingers, and swung his boots to find support.

The movement weakened his hold, and he lost his grip.

Sliding down, he tried to catch something, anything to stop his momentum.

He landed with a thud; the air knocked from his lungs.

Dizziness flooded his brain.

The sound of barking dogs grew louder, louder.

A memory clouded his thoughts: sharp teeth ripping through his jacket, his flesh. He cried out in pain.

No one heard him. He was alone, at the mercy of his enemies.

And he would die.

Embarrassment flushed Rose's cheeks. She knew Oscar, her border collie-golden retriever mix, had a mind of his own, but she also knew he had a strong play drive, which should technically make him a good search-and-rescue dog. He certainly wore the SAR training vest proudly.

After today's failed test, she and everyone else with Northwest Montana Search and Rescue knew the truth: Oscar had a long way to go to qualify.

"Let's call it a day," team leader Simon Washburn said into his radio to the rest of his team.

Right, how many hours could Rose expect the SAR volunteers to hide out in the cold, waiting for Oscar to get his act together and find them? It had been three hours and he wasn't any closer to catching scent as when they'd first started the exercise.

"I'm really sorry, Simon," Rose offered.

"It's okay." The fifty-something team leader gave Oscar a friendly pet. "Maybe SAR isn't his thing."

"I'd like to try again, after I've worked with him more."

"We have another qualification challenge next month. I'll put you and Oscar at the top of the list. In the meantime, we could always use an extra human on our searches."

"Count me in."

Oscar's ears pricked, and a low rumble resonated from his throat.

Uh-oh.

"Leave it," she ordered her dog.

Instead, he took off running.

"Oscar, no!"

She glanced at Simon.

"Go on, you'd better retrieve the retriever," Simon said.

"Don't wait for us." She ran after her smart but obstinate dog. "Oscar, right here!"

Instead of returning to her side, he disappeared around a turn up ahead. The border collie part of Oscar made him whip-fast and once he set his goal on getting somewhere, no one could catch him.

"I'm going to put you in your crate and take away Mr. Aardvark!" she shouted, in hot pursuit. She wouldn't crate him, but some days she wanted to, if nothing else to protect Oscar from himself. He assumed the world loved him, didn't sense danger when he pestered the horses who could easily kick him by accident. If that wasn't bad enough, if the two-year-old pup wasn't properly entertained he'd make his own entertainment in the form of shredding important documents or gnawing on the wood furniture. Although her mom suggested he'd outgrow the mischievous behavior, Rose wasn't so sure.

Rose had trained plenty of dogs for her clients, but Oscar, a mix fondly referred to as a coltriever, was a special breed that proved her biggest challenge.

"Cookie! Cookie!" she shouted, hoping a treat would entice him to return before he ran all the way to Missoula.

Nothing.

She didn't get it. Oscar was a sweet-natured dog, mostly obedient and good with kids. Why was his purpose in life so hard to figure out? Rose assumed he had a special purpose considering his origins. Oscar shouldn't have survived the neglect he'd suffered at a puppy mill. He'd nearly died at the vet's office, but he and his four siblings recovered and were adopted out. Oscar's adoptive family had hired Rose to train the pup, but once it became obvious Oscar had way too much energy for their family, they asked Rose to find a more suitable home for him.

With one look into those caramel-colored eyes, Rose fell instantly in love with the canine.

A part of her identified with Oscar, the runt of the litter, the baby, like Rose. He was an anomaly since his siblings were easily trained. She'd enjoyed working with them and their families. At one point she'd even considered training Oscar and offering him to another family but found she couldn't part with the coltriever.

"Oscar! C'mon, buddy! Right here!" Her voice cracked with worry that he'd pick a fight with a wild animal.

Like a bear.

Please, God, help me find him.

Rose didn't think she could survive more loss on top of the death of her sister nearly two years ago, and her recent breakup with T.J. When not getting into trouble, Oscar was the best comfort in the world. If she had a particularly bad day, he'd lie across her lap and look at her with those soulful eyes, comforting her in a way that took the edge off her grief, her anxiety.

A piercing whine echoed across the trail. She gasped. Oscar had done it. He'd gone after the wrong playmate and was hurt.

"Oscar! Where are you, buddy?"

Another whine was followed by a soft bark.

Had he been injured so badly he couldn't release a full-throated bark?

She continued up the trail, trying to pinpoint his location. "Oscar, speak!"

Silence answered her.

Then the frantic dog burst through a cluster of Douglas fir trees and raced toward her. She sighed with relief, kneeled and opened her arms. Professionally speaking she shouldn't be condoning his bad behavior, but she couldn't help herself.

Oscar launched at her, nearly knocking her over. She hugged him, burying her face in his fur.

"Good boy, good boy," she repeated. Since dogs only remembered the most recent action, she pulled a cookie out of her pocket. "Here ya go."

Oddly, he ignored the cookie and took off again. What on earth? She stood. "Hey!"

He stopped short of the trees, turned and barked at her. A full-throated, pointed bark.

"Okay, okay, what is it?" She closed the distance between them.

He spun around and disappeared into the forest. Both border collies and golden retrievers were smart dogs, and Rose's training philosophy was to respect the animal's individuality and instincts.

Since she knew Oscar wasn't hurt, she clicked into training mode and focused on interpreting his behavior. Pushing through the cluster of trees, she heard Oscar's odd whining sound again.

"Oscar, where are you, buddy?" she called out.

A low, rumbly bark answered her. Man, she hoped he hadn't found a wounded animal she'd have to shoot to put it out of its misery. Pops taught her to always carry a pistol in case she needed to show mercy in the face of anguish.

Another insistent whine drew her attention to the right. She followed the sound, now more frantic. She scanned the area...

And saw her coltriever in a perfect doggy sit, whimpering over what looked like a body.

A dead body?

She reached for her radio as she approached. Although the person was facedown, she noted men's boots, a dark brown jacket and hoodie sticking out of the collar. She decided to check for a pulse to determine if she could offer first aid or if it was too late for that.

She took a few steps closer. The man groaned and turned over.

Oscar barked.

The man scrambled away from Oscar, backing up against a boulder. His chest heaved in and out and his eyes watered with fear.

He was afraid of Oscar?

"It's okay. He won't hurt you," Rose said.

The stranger couldn't take his eyes off Oscar.

Rose had never seen that look before—beyond terror—and felt horrible that her dog was causing the reaction.

"Oscar, right here," she said.

He didn't obey at first, probably confused as to why the stranger wasn't happy to see him, praising him, petting him. In Rose's experience, dogs sensed when a human was uncomfortable by their presence, making the dog more determined to win him over.

"Chick-chick," Rose said, her special communication, and Oscar looked at her.

"Right here," she said firmly.

Oscar trotted to her side and sat, looking up into her eyes for his next direction.

"Good boy." She stroked his silky fur and offered him a cookie. He happily chomped it, then turned back to the stranger. "Leave it," she said.

The man's bright blue eyes were no longer fixated on Oscar. Instead, they had turned glassy, his back rigid against the rock, as if something was right in front of him, threatening him. She wished Jacob, her niece's dad, was here. As a former therapist, he'd know how to help this guy. The man looked to be in his thirties, with a slight beard, but she couldn't tell the color of his hair since he wore a navy blue knit cap.

He seemed frozen in place, unable to communicate. Or was it more than that? Had he been injured and needed SAR? If that was the case, time was critical. She considered ways to encourage him to talk to her. She remembered how Jacob would calm her niece, Miri, by speaking softly, telling stories to distract her from brewing anxiety.

"I'm Rose," she said, still petting Oscar's thick fur. "This is Oscar. We're out here training for search-and-rescue. Why are you here?"

He stared straight ahead. Didn't answer.

She watched his chest rise and fall with each breath. Okay, so he was breathing more fully. That was a good sign.

"Unfortunately, Oscar totally failed his test today, didn't you, buddy?" She looked at her black pup with white paws, partially white snout and soul patch that made him look older than his two years. He blinked adoring eyes at her. "But we don't give up that easy."

She kneeled and gave Oscar a hug. "I think he was distracted on our practice mission because he sensed you were out here." She looked at the stranger. "He was worried about you."

The man's gaze slowly turned to Oscar, but the stranger's eyes were still wide with fear. She knew it wouldn't help to tell him the dog was harmless. The feeling of fear was very real, and was sometimes triggered by the past. She didn't want the man's fear to prevent him from getting help, so she decided to try again, try to make a connection.

"I'm Rose, and you are…?"

He didn't respond.

"Can you at least tell me if you're hurt?"

Nothing.

She glanced up through the thick trees surrounding them. It would be dark in an hour, making it more dangerous to be out here amid the wild animals of Montana.

"Okay, well, I'm going to call for backup." She pressed the button on her radio.

"Please," the man said.

His deep, hoarse voice stopped her cold.

"Oh good, you're okay," she said. "You *are* okay, right?"

He blinked. Didn't answer.

"How long have you been out here? What's your name?" she said.

No response.

"Oh man, head injury? You don't remember your name? I'd better get help." She pressed the button. "Simon—"

"Don't… Please don't tell them where I am," he interrupted.

"I'm just calling for help," she said.

He shook his head. Panicked. She noticed his hands were trembling. He fisted them, either to stop the involuntary reaction or to hide it from her, she wasn't sure.

"I don't want to upset you, but you need help," she offered.

He glared at her with anger in his eyes. Now *that* she didn't expect.

"Unless you can walk on your own?"

The anger softened and he nodded. "I can walk."

"Good. Let's go, then, before it gets dark." She gave Oscar the command to stay back in order to give the man space and not upset him further.

The stranger closed his eyes, took a deep breath and held it. Then he exhaled slowly through his mouth. He did this a few times. She assumed it was a breathing technique to calm down his fight-or-flight response. He certainly wouldn't get far if his body was trembling with fear and adrenaline.

She didn't rush him, figuring this had happened to him before and he'd developed ways to cope.

Like Rose had after her sister had died in a car accident two years ago. Although Rose's coping skills could use improvement since she was haunted by the thought that the wrong sister had died. Cassie had a child who needed her, whereas Rose hadn't much to show for her twenty-eight years but an inability to find her calling and make a difference in the world. She shook off the self-recrimination.

Let go; let God. The mantra often grounded her.

The stranger slowly stood, leaning against the

boulder for support. This guy wouldn't get very far if he could barely stand.

Rose realized that, similar to dealing with a traumatized horse, she had to earn this man's trust in order to effectively help him.

Adjusting his backpack, he took a few steps.

In the wrong direction.

"The trail is back this way," she said.

He turned to her. "They'll find me if I take the trail."

"Who?"

Without answering, he continued walking away from her and stumbled. Rose rushed to his side and gripped his arm to help him remain steady. When he glanced at her, Rose's breath caught at the look of defeat in his eyes. She knew that look. She'd seen it in the mirror.

"Hey, you're going be okay," she said.

He pulled away and continued toward the dense forest. He wasn't thinking clearly, paranoid about someone out to get him.

"Please, sir, going that way isn't a good idea. Let me—"

A gunshot echoed through the forest.

The stranger dropped to the ground and Rose dived for cover.

TWO

As Rose scrambled for a better, hidden position behind a boulder, she considered that a hunter could have fired the shot or…

The stranger wasn't being paranoid after all, and someone was after him.

"Oscar, right here," she said. Instead, the coltriever plopped down next to the man.

She pressed the button on the radio. "Simon, this is Rose. Someone's shooting at us, over."

She blocked out the racing, fear-driven chatter in her brain. It didn't help to panic when she needed every ounce of good sense to stay safe.

To keep the man with the piercing blue eyes alive.

"Who's shooting, over?" Simon responded.

"I don't know. About a quarter mile from where you and I split up I found an injured hiker and was helping him when I heard a gunshot and he dropped to the ground. I think—" she hesitated "—I think he might have been hit, over."

"Roger, we're on the way."

"Bring sheriff's deputies, people with firearms, over."

"We are all packing. Aren't you, over?"

"Affirmative, over."

"Be there soon, over."

Sure, she had her pistol, but hadn't planned on using it, especially not on a person. She peered around the boulder looking for the source of the gunfire.

If the shooter was still out there...

He would no doubt come for the vulnerable man on the ground in plain view. She clipped the radio onto her belt. She wanted to get the guy out of sight before the shooter tried again.

That is, if the enigmatic stranger was capable of moving and hadn't been injured. There was one way to find out.

"Oscar, speak," she commanded.

The dog barked, she repeated the command, and he barked again.

The stranger's eyes popped open, and he scrambled to get away from Oscar. That was Rose's plan: have Oscar herd the guy toward Rose to safety.

"Good dog," she said, pulling her gun from its holster. She wanted to be ready, just in case.

Thinking it was a game, Oscar kept barking, charging and retreating until the man was close enough for Rose to grab. She helped pull him out of sight.

"Oscar, quiet," she commanded. "Back up." She put out her hand. Oscar did as ordered and waited for further instruction. The stranger's eyes were pinched shut.

"Sorry about the dog," she apologized. "I needed to get you out of range. Were you hit?"

He blinked his eyes open, looking at her with confusion.

"Were you shot?" she said.

He shook his head that he was not.

"Good." She sighed with relief.

Oscar whined and the man jerked.

"Oscar, quiet," she said.

The dog lay down with a harrumph and a great big sigh.

Although unable to identify the exact origin of the shot, she knew it wasn't behind them since that area was mostly trees and the mountain wall. She scanned 180 degrees in front of her, looking for the shooter.

"I'm sorry."

She snapped her attention to the stranger. "What?"

"That you're in danger...because of me," he said.

She wasn't sure what surprised her more, that he spoke in the first place or that he was offering a lucid response: regret.

"What's your name?" she said.

He didn't respond.

She turned back to surveying the area. "I think

I've at least earned the privilege of knowing your name."

Silence.

Okay, so maybe this guy was into something shady and was hiding from authorities. In which case he'd want to keep his identity private. Fine by Rose. Her job was to help him, not judge him.

A few tense minutes passed, and Rose focused on the upside of this harrowing experience. Oscar had actually found someone, and more importantly, this man wouldn't die out here in the wilderness, abandoned and alone.

Like her sister, Cassie, whose life ended on the side of a highway as motorists passed by, not realizing two people were dying in an overturned car.

"Noah," the man said.

She glanced over her shoulder. "Excuse me?"

"My name is Noah."

"Nice to meet you, Noah." She nodded toward her dog. "Sorry about my ill-behaved but kindhearted dog, Oscar. I sense you're not a dog person, but he's the reason I found you. It it weren't for him, you'd still be unconscious and an easy target for whoever is shooting at you."

Noah glanced at the dog. Oscar wagged his tail.

"Who *is* shooting at us, by the way?" she said.

His gaze dropped and he went silent again.

Oscar's ears pricked. He growled a low, throaty sound. Noah clenched his jaw.

"He's not growling at you," she whispered. "He

hears something. Oscar, quiet." She pressed her fingers to her lips, took a deep breath and closed her eyes to enhance her other senses.

There. The sound of men talking.

She glanced at Noah's taut expression. He must have heard it, too. Leaning against the boulder, she cocked her head to determine their location. The sound of their voices increased.

"He should be right around here somewhere."

The voice was close, she guessed less than a hundred feet away.

"You better not have shot him," another man said. "We need him alive."

"I fired a round to scare him."

"You're an idiot. Greene! C'mon out! We won't hurt you!"

Rose adjusted her grip on the pistol. It was an automatic so she could fire multiple times, but she'd never shot a person and had hoped to avoid that experience altogether.

"We need to get you back to the center where we can straighten this out!" the man called.

She checked her phone. Good, she had reception. She texted Simon asking him to hurry, and to have the dogs bark as they approached. She hoped barking would make the men scatter.

Then she did the only thing she could: she prayed.

This would definitely go down as one of the craziest days of her life: trying to get her dog qualified for SAR, and ending up protecting a man who was being stalked and shot at. Yet it didn't sound like the aggressors wanted to kill him. No, they wanted to take him back to the "center." Which meant what? Noah was suffering from a mental disorder? No, they wouldn't send such violent men to retrieve him if that were the case.

The sound of barking dogs intensified across the landscape.

"Did you hear that?" one of the men said. "Dogs, let's go."

"What about—"

"Now! No one can know we're here."

Rose counted to sixty and peered around the boulder. She spotted the backs of two men heading up the trail. One wore a black jacket, the other olive green. She wished she could have gotten a better look so she could describe facial features to police.

Although they were going in the opposite direction of where she and Noah would rendezvous with SAR, she didn't want to take any chances. She needed to distance herself and Noah from their attackers.

"Can you walk?" she asked Noah.

He stood but was a little wobbly. When she reached out to assist, he put up his hand to decline her offer.

"We should stay off the trail for a bit," she said.

He nodded.

Using the trees as cover, she led him in the opposite direction of their pursuers. Oscar raced up ahead, enthusiastically sniffing the ground. Once she was confident they were far enough away from the shooters, she decided to start a dialogue.

"Don't suppose you want to tell me who those guys were?" She glanced at him.

He didn't answer, didn't even nod this time.

"Are you from this area?" she said.

"Virginia."

"I'm assuming that's where this *center* place is?"

"Yes."

"Are you…a patient there?"

He shot her a look.

"Too intrusive? Yeah, too intrusive." She started to help him navigate a cluster of rocks and stopped herself because he obviously didn't want to be physically helped. "You can't blame me for asking. I put myself in danger for you. Well, actually, Oscar put himself in danger and I went to help Oscar because he was making this strange whining sound that I'd never heard before, and I thought he found a wounded animal or something." She knew she was rambling but couldn't help it. It was a distraction from her anxiety.

Anxiety triggered by danger, by threat.

By dark memories from her own past that even prayer hadn't completely dissolved.

"The search-and-rescue team will transport you back to town. Don't be surprised if they bring a sheriff's deputy since I reported shots fired. Which means police will want a statement."

"I have nothing to say."

"No kidding." The smart comment slipped out because she was still on high alert, and when Rose felt anxious she not only chatted away, but she also tended to blurt out the raw, unfiltered truth. Sometimes with an edge.

She studied Noah, who was doing his breathing exercise again, a deep inhale, followed by a slow exhale.

"Don't worry. Those guys went in the opposite direction," she offered to comfort him.

He kept breathing, in and out. Her words didn't seem to help.

"So, you're from Virginia," she started, hoping to distract him from his fear. "I was born and raised in Boulder Creek, moved away at twenty, did some college, and lived in Boise, Portland and most recently Seattle. Returned to Montana a few years ago to help my family after my sister died."

He glanced at her, expectant.

"Car accident." She turned back to their makeshift trail. "I figured Mom and Dad needed me more than I needed to enjoy life in the city. I'll hang around until I feel like it's the right time to leave. I'd hoped to pursue a degree in education, but since coming back I've started a successful business training dogs and taking care of people's homes. I guess you wouldn't know I can train dogs considering how miserably I'm failing with Oscar."

"Why do you say that?" Noah said.

Again, a bit shocked that he'd spoken, she hesitated before answering.

"Too intrusive?" he said, repeating her words.

Was that a sense of humor? If so, that meant he'd gone from terrified to lighthearted in only a few minutes, which made her uncomfortable. She was never sure when her ex-boyfriend from Seattle would shift moods from loving to critical, or why. Since that breakup three years ago, she craved stability and avoided the unexpected.

Yet here she was, helping a stranger who was being shot at.

"About Oscar," she continued. "If I'd done a better job training him, he would have qualified for search-and-rescue today."

"He found me."

"Yes, but finding you wasn't the goal. His mission was to find a well-placed team member. Instead, he couldn't focus because he was distracted by your presence for some reason. I guess that's a good thing."

"You guess?"

"Obviously it was a good thing he found you, but I was hoping he'd find an SAR team member so he would have qualified. But Oscar's got a mind of his own. He's gotta do it his way."

"I can relate."

She glanced at him. "You're a rebel too, huh?"

He shrugged.

"Is that why people are after you?"

"I can't talk about it and risk putting you in danger."

"Why, thank you, but I think it's too late for that."

The chatty woman made a clicking sound and the dog returned to her side. She gave him a hearty pat on the head, made a hand motion, and he took off again, ahead of them.

The tension in Noah's shoulders eased a bit. He had to get over his fear of dogs; fear of being hunted…killed. He wouldn't survive another day carrying the weight of this oppressive trauma on his shoulders.

He wouldn't have survived at all if it hadn't been for this woman and her dog.

Rose. The name suited her with her rosy cheeks, bright green catlike eyes and confident attitude.

Noah still couldn't believe how she'd taken charge of the situation, kept him safe and out of harm's way. What kind of woman did that? Put herself at risk for someone else? For a stranger?

"You shouldn't be doing this," he blurted out.

She shot him a look he couldn't interpret.

"You're welcome?" She continued to push aside brush so they could stay hidden while hiking.

"You could have been seriously injured."

"And you could have been hurt worse if I'd left you there. What did those guys want anyway? What's this center place all about?"

It was too complicated to explain, especially to a stranger whom he'd known for twenty minutes. Besides, trust was foreign to Noah.

"I shouldn't tell you," he said. "It could put you in danger."

"Like I said before, too late for that. Okay, Noah, from Virginia, if you won't tell me about the center, how about at least sharing what brought you to this part of the country."

"You ask a lot of questions."

"I'm a curious person. Used to be a reporter for my high school newspaper. Long time ago, but some instincts stick with you."

Instincts, yeah. Noah knew about those, trusted them, and his instincts were clear about Rose from Boulder Creek: she was not a threat. She'd saved his life, and it wouldn't hurt to have one person on his side going forward. Was it fair to put her life in further danger?

"I guess that's why I didn't leave you out there to be picked off like a duck in a shooting gallery at the county fair," she continued. "Instinct told me you needed help, and that's what we do in the Rogers family, we help people."

"Strangers?"

"Sure, why not?"

"You don't know me or my situation."

"I know enough."

"Meaning?"

"When Oscar and I found you, you were suffering from a post-traumatic episode. I wouldn't be much of a Christian if I'd abandoned you to your fear and your enemies."

"A Christian," he said, his voice flat. He'd seen enough violence in the world to believe God didn't exist.

"Yes. The kind of Christian who walks the walk. You know, what would Jesus do in any given situation."

"Oh."

"I sense that's not your thing?"

"No, ma'am."

The woman's radio beeped. "Rose, we're by Barton Rock. Where are you, over?"

"Off trail. We'll head down and connect with you in about ten minutes, over."

"Roger that. You okay, over?"

"Yes, we're both unharmed, over." She shoved the radio back on her belt.

Noah was unharmed thanks to this brave woman and her dog. A woman who didn't seem the least bit fazed by the events of the past twenty minutes.

"You've been shot at before?" he said.

"No, and I'd like to avoid that experience in the future, thank-you-very-much. Then again, they weren't shooting at me, they were shooting at you."

She glanced at him, her cheeks rosy and eyes bright. He sensed she loved the outdoors.

"It sounded like they weren't out to kill you, just catch you?" She shook her head. "Stupid criminals. They usually are, you know. Stupid, I mean."

"You have experience with criminals?"

"I used to date a police detective. I heard stories."

"Used to?"

"Nah-uh. I'm not sharing anything about my failed love life to a guy who won't even tell me what he's doing out here."

"Maybe I needed to get away."

She shot him a skeptical look.

"I'm looking for a friend," he admitted.

"Out here?"

"Yes. He owns a cabin off the grid, west of Boulder Creek."

"There's nothing where you were headed except a mountain range. I doubt there are any cabins." She eyed him. "No roads."

Which is exactly how Thomas had described

his paradise: a remote cabin nestled in the snowy mountains of Montana with a view that took your breath away.

"If he's a friend, wouldn't he have given you better directions than turn left at Boulder Creek?" she asked.

He didn't have specific directions because Thomas didn't know Noah was looking for him, along with the Feds, and the guys claiming to be from the center. Or did he? Was that why Thomas was hiding in the mountains?

Noah hoped his friend had intentionally disappeared and hadn't been terminated by the enemy. The enemy? Noah wasn't in Afghanistan anymore.

But there *was* an enemy out there, poised to strike, and it wouldn't hurt for Noah to think like a soldier in order to defend himself.

And the woman who'd rescued him.

"Where are you staying?" she asked.

Good question. He'd planned to camp his way to Thomas's cabin, then bunk with him. Noah didn't think he'd be attacked before he even got to the pass.

"I was going to camp."

She hesitated and looked up at the darkening sky. "Not sure that's a great idea considering the weather, and your condition."

"My condition?"

"You're a little unsteady on your feet, plus the

post-traumatic terrors might throw off your judgment."

"Tell me what you really think."

"I just did." She winked at him.

Winked? This woman was…unusual.

Noah had dated a few women since he'd returned to civilian life, but none could deal with the inconsistency of his personality: a loving, kind man one minute; a terrified soldier the next. It was asking too much for any woman to commit to that kind of instability. Noah knew it, and although his last serious girlfriend talked a good game, in the end he always felt he'd failed her somehow because he couldn't control the timing of his episodes or his mood swings. It's not like he wanted to drift into the darkness. But sometimes it crept up on him and no matter how hard he tried, he couldn't tamp it down.

"If you can't find a room in town, we've got a few vacant guest cabins at the ranch."

"The ranch?"

"My family owns the Boulder Creek Guest Ranch."

"You'd let me stay there after what happened today?"

"It's actually up to Mom and Dad, but we have experience helping people in danger. Besides, some of our cabins are a good distance from the main house. Kind of remote." She offered a slight smile. "You look like a remote type of guy."

Her dog started barking and she glanced up ahead.

A remote type of guy. Yep, she nailed it. He'd been remote since he'd returned from service, which was why he struggled to maintain relationships.

Thomas, his army buddy, sensed Noah was flailing and helped him back on track, encouraged him to finish his degree and secured him a job interview in IT security with Stratosphere, where Thomas was a manager.

"Besides, I still have pull with the PD," the woman continued.

"Excuse me?" He'd lost track of their conversation.

"After T.J. does a background check and you come up clean, there's no reason *not* to let you stay at the ranch."

"T.J.?"

"My ex, the detective? It's the least he can do considering everything that happened between us. Whoops, wasn't going to talk about that. You will come up clean, right?"

"Yes, ma'am."

At least he hoped so. He wasn't sure if Thomas's enemies, now Noah's enemies by association, could manipulate data to make it look like Noah was guilty of criminal activity. He'd be arrested and the Stratosphere Center would bail him out and have complete control over him.

"Is that a definite yes or a maybe yes?" she said.

"Excuse me?"

"You...don't have a criminal record, do you?"

"No, ma'am."

"'Cuz for a second there you looked like you weren't sure."

"I'm sure."

"Rose, where are you, over?" a man's voice squawked through her radio.

"Be there in five minutes, over."

Noah instinctively slowed. He didn't want anyone to see him, didn't want the police to question him. How would he explain what he was doing out here being chased by armed gunmen?

Her dog took off in a determined sprint.

"Oscar! Get back here! He must have seen the search team. Hey, what's wrong?" she asked Noah.

Noah shook his head.

"You'll be safe with the SAR team."

"I...can't."

"Can't what?"

"Talk to people."

"Yeah, well, I'm a chatty Cathy so I'll do the talking. C'mon."

He scanned his surroundings, looking for options. There weren't many, and he'd never make his way back to the original trail he thought led to Thomas's place in the dark of night.

"Sometimes you have to face your fears to

make them stop haunting you," she said. "Or at least trust somebody to help you through."

She took a step toward him and extended her purple-gloved hand.

As he looked at it, another image popped into his mind: Thomas, extending his gloved hand to help Noah up and out of the line of fire. Maybe it was okay to accept help from this spirited woman.

Noah glanced into Rose's green eyes. She offered a half smile.

He took her hand…

…felt a twinge of hope, hope that maybe he'd make it to town and stay alive one more day.

Back at the sheriff's office, Rose's ex-boyfriend, Detective T. J. Harper, tried to separate her and Noah to get their statements. She didn't want to leave Noah alone given his emotional state and the fear still coloring his eyes.

Rose knew what it felt like to be mired in panic, sucked into a vortex of fear and darkness. She spent plenty of time trying to conquer her trauma, and knew that helping others went a long way to redirecting the panic and not getting pulled into the past.

Into victimhood.

Into reliving the event.

"You were out there with search-and-rescue?" Detective Harper asked Rose.

"Yes."

"But you were alone when you found Mr. Greene?"

"I was chasing after Oscar, who had found Noah. We were helping him when someone started shooting at us."

"Why would they shoot at you?" He directed his question to Noah.

"I don't know, sir."

"That's not good enough. They could have shot Rose. I want answers!"

"Detective, can I have a word?" Rose stood and motioned T.J. into the hallway.

She worried T.J.'s aggressive questioning might trigger Noah's trauma.

T.J. shut the door to the conference room and looked at her. "What?"

"Go easy on him," she said.

"My gut tells me something is way off here."

"What you're sensing is that he suffers from PTSD. He's a veteran."

"And you were with him because...?"

"I wasn't *with* him, T.J. Like I said, Oscar and I found him. Did you do a background check?" She held her breath.

"He's clean."

She exhaled, relieved.

"He's still a threat, Rose."

"I don't think he's dangerous."

"Why? Because he's wounded and needed help? That's no reason to trust him."

"Noah said he's looking for his friend Thomas, who he thinks has a cabin west of Boulder Creek."

"That's not my concern. My concern is that someone was shooting at him and could have hit you."

"I'm fine."

"You could have been hurt, seriously hurt."

There it was: guilt. T.J. felt guilty about Rose's older sister's death, and had tried to make up for it by taking care of Rose. Rose thought genuine affection had motivated him to date her. She'd been wrong.

Protecting her, managing her, taking care of her. An old story—everyone taking care of Rosie the baby—that she thought she'd left behind when she'd moved away.

"I appreciate your concern. I do," she said. "Believe it or not, I can take care of myself."

"Rose—"

"Are we nearly done? Oscar is going to rip apart the inside of my truck if I don't get him dinner soon."

T.J. studied her for a second, sighed, then opened the conference room door. She joined Noah at the table.

"Do you have anything else that can help me find the shooters?" T.J. asked. "Did they call each other by name or say something to help us identify them?"

"I heard something." She hesitated and glanced at Noah, who nodded for her to continue. "They talked about wanting Noah alive to take him back to the center."

"The center?" T.J. directed his question at Noah.

"I work at the Stratosphere Center in Virginia."

"What kind of work do you do?"

"Tech security."

"If I call your company, will they confirm your employment?"

"Yes, sir, although I notified HR I'd be gone for a while."

"And they sent armed gunmen all the way to Montana to bring you back? Something doesn't add up here, Mr. Greene."

Noah studied his hands in his lap.

There was a knock on the door and a secretary poked her head into the room. "Sorry to interrupt but I've got someone on the line who claims to have seen two men fitting the description of the shooters."

"I'll be right there." T.J. turned to Noah. "Mr. Greene, I'd prefer you keep your distance from residents of Boulder Creek." He shot a quick glance at Rose. "It's my job to protect them and I'd hate to see this business of yours put any of my people in harm's way."

"I understand, sir."

"A deputy will give you a ride to a motel within the hour."

"Thank you, sir."

T.J. left the conference room.

"He's your ex?" Noah said.

Rose nodded.

"He still cares about you." Noah shot her a look, like the words had escaped by accident.

"We'll always care about each other, I suppose. It's complicated."

"Usually is."

She stood. "C'mon, I'll drop you at a motel."

"The detective said—"

"There's one on my way home. Who knows how long you'll have to wait for a ride." She led Noah into the hallway. T.J. was nowhere in sight, so she could avoid a lecture about giving Noah a ride.

By the time they got to her truck, Oscar was practically bouncing off the ceiling he was so excited to see them.

Noah didn't return the sentiment. She noticed his clenched jaw and she told Oscar to be quiet. He obeyed with a disappointed whine.

"Hey, I've got another idea," Rose said. "I called my parents, and they said the Glacier Cabin is still available."

"No, thank you."

"It has running water and a toilet if that's what you're worried about." She pulled onto the highway.

"The detective said to keep my distance from locals. I don't want to end up in jail."

"He can't put you in jail for renting a cabin at the Ranch."

"They can do whatever they want," he said, his voice weaker than a minute ago.

"They? You mean cops?"

He didn't answer.

"Trust me, T.J.'s bark is bigger than his bite. He would never abuse his power as a detective."

Noah gazed out the window. He seemed lost, like he'd given up on finding his friend, maybe even given up on himself. She believed every human had a God-given purpose, and to not share that gift with the world was the real tragedy.

Even if Rose struggled to find hers. Some days she felt like she was moving in the right direction, while other days it felt like she was running from commitment.

From her mistakes she thought she'd put behind her. She wondered what mistakes haunted Noah.

"You're in tech security?" she said.

"Yes."

"How did you know that's what you wanted to do?"

"I didn't. Thomas suggested it."

"He sounds like a good man."

He pointed to a motel in the distance. "What about that one?"

"Are you sure you don't want to stay at the ranch? One or two nights? It will give you time to relax in a safe environment."

"There is no such place."

Whoa, he was certainly tortured by his past. Maybe Jacob, her niece's dad and a licensed mental health counselor who lived at the ranch, could help Noah. She'd make it a point to find him tonight and ask his advice.

"Please drop me off there," he said.

"But—"

"Please, Rose."

He hadn't called her by name before, and it startled her. She wasn't sure why.

Oscar whined from the back seat and she wondered if he'd picked up on a change in Noah's voice. She certainly didn't want to create more stress and trigger another episode.

"Okay, if you're sure," she said.

"I am."

"Please know you're always welcome. If you change your mind—"

"I won't."

His words sounded so final. Why did she care so much? She didn't know him that well.

But he was obviously in a fragile emotional state and might not be equipped to make the best decisions. Cassie had been in emotional turmoil when she got into a car with a man she knew had been overserved.

This wasn't Cassie. Noah was a stranger looking for his friend in the mountains. End of story.

Only, something bothered her.

She pulled up to the Greystone Motel and he got out of the truck. Oscar started doing an anxious dance in the back seat.

"Oscar, stop," she said.

Noah grabbed his backpack off the floor.

"Hey, do you have a phone?" She motioned for him to pass it to her. "I'll add my number to your contacts."

When he wavered, she said, "In case you have questions about the area. I'm not asking for yours, so you won't have to worry about me calling you. I do have a life, you know."

He pulled a phone out of his jacket and offered it to her. She added her number to his contacts and handed it back. "I'm being sincere when I say don't hesitate to call. I hope you find your friend. God bless."

He hesitated a second, then shut the door and walked toward the lobby of the motel. Oscar whined in protest.

"Yeah, I know, buddy."

She tried surrendering her worry about Noah. He seemed so lost, and too proud to accept help. He was also very direct.

He still cares about you, Noah had commented about T.J.

More like guilt for not having saved Rose's sister. If Rose had pursued a serious relationship with T.J., she'd always wonder if his intentions were pure, or if they were born out of his need for redemption.

He couldn't save Cassie, so he'd marry her little sister to make things right. A warped way of thinking in Rose's mind, but grief had a way of warping perceptions. Ever since Cassie's death, Rose had done enough soul-searching to know she didn't want to live a life driven by grief. She wanted to share God's glory through love and joy.

She drove for a few minutes, finally taking a deep breath as she processed all that had happened. Word must have gotten back to her family about the day's events. She was about to check in with Mom when her phone rang with an incoming call. She didn't recognize the number.

She pressed the accept button. "Hello?"

No one spoke. Scuffling sounds echoed through the audio system of her truck.

"Is someone there?"

More scuffling, a thud and the sound of a man groaning. It had to be a mistake, a wrong number.

"You had enough, Greene?"

She glared at her phone.

"C'mon, let's finish this," another man said.

"Noah!" she shouted.

The call dropped.

THREE

"You shouldn't have run from us," the tall guy standing over Noah said.

Okay, so these were the guys from earlier, sent by Stratosphere.

"Where's Thomas?" the short and stocky guy demanded.

"I don't know."

He kicked Noah in the gut. He coughed, struggled to breathe.

"Give us Thomas's location and we'll walk away."

Sure, and leave Noah's dead body behind. Given Noah's history of struggling with PTSD, if his body was found in a random motel room in Montana, people would assume he killed himself.

"He called someone," the short guy said.

The men hovered over him, analyzing his phone. Noah peered through slightly closed eyes, wanting to create a mental picture in his head so he could report their description to authorities.

If he made it out of this room alive.

The tall guy got in his face. "Who'd you call, soldier? Who's on the way to help you?"

"They'll be too late," the short guy said.

The tall guy grabbed Noah's jacket. "Who!"

Noah glared, clenching his jaw.

"I got this." The stocky guy pulled Noah to his feet.

He noted the man's brown eyes and a scar along his jawline. He'd no doubt been in battle.

"Did you call your buddy? Did you call Thomas?"

Noah shook his head that he hadn't. Stocky Guy delivered a backhanded slap that made Noah's cheek sting.

"Who's coming?"

Noah hadn't made a call, didn't have time to…

Rose. She'd been the last one to touch his phone when she'd added her number. What if he'd accidentally called her and she heard what was happening, heard him being assaulted?

She'd feel compelled to act. To rescue him again.

Stocky Guy got in Noah's face. "Doesn't matter who shows up. We'll take care of him."

Him? No, not him. Her. Rose was coming.

Which meant…

Fury exploded in Noah's chest. He headbutted Stocky Guy and fired off multiple punches to his gut. Stunned, it took the tall guy a few seconds to react. He went for a concealed firearm and Noah charged, slamming him against the wall. Noah grabbed the gun, pistol-whipped him and fled the motel room, hoping to find safety long enough to call Rose and tell her not to return to the motel.

Then he realized he'd lost his phone while grappling with his attackers.

He sprinted to the motel office.

"I need your phone," he blurted out.

The older woman's eyes widened.

"Please!" He had minutes, maybe seconds, before they found him and dragged him away. And if this woman witnessed that kidnapping, her life was in danger, too.

She placed the phone on the counter and stepped back.

"You'd better hide." He grabbed the phone and realized he didn't have Rose's number. He called 9-1-1.

The woman at the front desk darted through a door into a back office.

"9-1-1, what is your emergency?"

"Rose, Rose is in danger," Noah said.

"What is your emergency, sir?"

"I'm at the—"

He was grabbed from behind by a firm arm wrapped around his neck. He kicked and swung his arms, but the guy had the advantage and wrestled Noah to the ground. Someone ripped off Noah's jacket and pushed up his sleeve.

A needle pricked his skin, the burn rushing up his arm. They'd drugged him. In a matter of minutes, he'd be neutralized, unable to defend himself.

"Get him up."

The stocky guy pulled Noah to his feet. Noah shoved the heel of his palm into the guy's face, breaking his nose, then side-kicked the tall guy in the groin.

Noah had to escape. Had to lead them away before the drug took effect. He sprinted out of the office toward the back of the property, hoping to use the trees as cover.

You've failed, soldier.

"No," he ground out. The trees that a moment ago were only a few feet away now seemed miles from reach.

You put others at risk. Innocent lives at risk.

"I didn't…didn't mean to…" He stumbled but recovered before he fell flat on his face.

One foot in front of the other. Slow and steady. It was Thomas's voice, leading Noah away from the carnage.

"Thomas," he uttered.

He needed his friend. Noah needed to know why, what happened. How Thomas got involved in something that forced him to go off the grid, something that put Noah's life in danger because he wanted to find him.

"Get him!" a male voice shouted.

A high-pitched wail made him stumble. They were close. Too close. He'd never make it.

* * *

Rose pulled into the motel lot and parked in the corner. Heart pounding, she watched, waited, and prayed deputies would arrive soon.

She called T.J. and it went into voice mail.

"It's Rose. You've got to get to the Greystone Motel before they kill him. I heard it—they were beating him. I'm here now. Hurry, T.J.!"

She ended the call and stared at the office. She'd already called dispatch, who said a unit was on the way because they'd received another call.

Rose fought the need to knock on every motel room door to find Noah. An unwise decision. What should she do?

After a moment of prayer, she sensed God's guidance: wait for authorities; and don't jump into the middle of a violent scene. Even though she carried a gun, threatening these men with it could go wrong in so many ways. They were brutal and violent. She was a dog trainer, a house manager.

She nervously tapped her fingers against the steering wheel. "C'mon, c'mon."

Oscar paced the back seat and whined.

"I know, buddy."

The muted sound of sirens echoed down the highway. Still too far away in her opinion.

The door to the motel office swung open and two men rushed out, furious. She ducked and watched through tinted windows as the men, she thought the same ones from earlier, marched toward a motel room and disappeared inside. A few seconds later they exited the room, one carrying a backpack.

Noah's backpack.

Why? Because he wouldn't need it anymore? She reached for the silver cross she wore around her neck.

The tall guy tossed Noah's pack into an SUV, and they took off. She made note of the make and model of the vehicle but couldn't clearly see the license plate from where she was parked.

Confident they were gone, she headed to the motel room. A part of her hoped Noah wasn't inside; a part of her hoped he was, and still alive.

She tapped on the door. "Noah?"

She turned the knob. It wasn't locked. She pushed open the door to a trashed room. It looked like a tornado had blown through it, upending furniture and ripping linens off the bed, obvious signs that Noah had fought his aggressors.

Then her gaze caught on a red stain on the wall beside the bathroom.

Blood.

"Noah," she hushed.

With a sigh, she took a step back out of the room and collided with a person.

She shrieked and spun around. T.J. glared at her. "You shouldn't have gone in there."

"Check the bathroom, see if he's in the tub or something," she ordered.

He hesitated, as if wanting to argue with her but thought better of it. "Stay here," he said, the edge in his voice softening.

She nodded.

T.J. disappeared into the room. As Rose paced, two patrol cars pulled into the motel lot, sirens blaring.

"Over here!" She motioned to them.

Oscar continued to bark furiously from her truck. "Quiet!" She made her hand signal and he stopped.

The deputies hopped out of their cars and joined her.

"Inside," she said. "T.J.—Detective Harper is in the room."

"Rose."

She turned to T.J., holding her breath.

"He's not in there."

"Who?" one of the deputies asked.

"The rescued hiker from earlier," T.J. said. "Deputy Long, take the motel clerk's statement. She called it in."

"Yes, sir."

"You've got to find him," Rose said to T.J. "He's hurt. I heard them—they were beating him up. They drove off in a dark SUV, a Chevy Equinox, I think. I didn't get the plate."

"Deputy Saunders, get Rose's statement and put out a bulletin on the SUV," T.J. said.

"There's no time. You have to find him." She

realized her voice was sounding desperate, panicked. She was reliving it: Mom's retelling of the
night Cassie had died.

Cassie didn't come home. No one knew where
she was.

She was right there all the time. On the side
of the road.

Dying.

"Rose, give Deputy Saunders as much detail
as you can, okay?"

She nodded, shoving back the bundle of emotions triggered by the thought that Noah was out
there, somewhere, fighting for his life.

Like Cassie.

Deputy Long jogged back toward them from
the motel office. "The clerk said the two guys
were angry when they left. She heard them curs-
ing from the other room."

"Maybe he got away," Rose said.

"Where, Rose? Where do you think he'd go?"
T.J. said.

"I… I don't know."

Her gaze drifted across the parking lot to her
truck, where Oscar burst into a new round of
barking almost as if he'd caught the scent of a
rabbit.

Or a man.

"Oscar can find him." She rushed to her truck.

"Rose, hang on," T.J. called out. "Let search-
and-rescue find him."

Waiting would put Noah at more risk. Who knew what they'd done to him and if the beating had triggered another traumatic episode. She put a harness on Oscar and hooked the lighted GPS beacon to his collar. "Find him, buddy."

She stepped out of his way and Oscar took off. She went after him. "He's around here, T.J., or Oscar wouldn't be so focused."

"Or he smelled a rabbit."

She dismissed his comment and continued to chase her dog. *Please, God, let him find Noah.*

The insurgents were sending the dogs again.

To find him.

To intimidate him.

To corner him.

Their sharp teeth ripping through his uniform, piercing his flesh.

"Let go, let go!" he cried out.

It was no use. He was pinned to the ground, unable to get up, unable to see clearly past the blur of terror.

"Over here!" one of them called to the others.

He was outnumbered. A dead man.

"Thomas!" he called. But Thomas wasn't there. Noah was alone. He'd die alone.

"Noah?" a soft voice said.

Soft, light, female.

"Noah, you're going to be okay."

It was a trick to get him to talk, to tell them

where his unit was located. He would resist, with all his might he would resist.

"No," he ground out.

"Noah, it's Rose. Rose and Oscar."

Someone placed his hand on a soft mass of fur.

"He found you again, see? He was worried and he found you."

He struggled to focus. At first he saw a silver cross hanging from a chain. Then his attention drifted up...

Into the most amazing, bright green eyes he'd ever seen. His heart slowed its racing beat, his mind cleared slightly.

"Rose," he said in a weak voice.

"It's okay. You're safe."

He sighed, all the tension leaving his body. Suddenly exhausted, he started to drift into a relaxed state. He knew he shouldn't let down his guard, but she was here. The green-eyed beauty had come to save him again.

The memory of how he'd ended up here rushed to the surface. Violent men threatening Thomas.

Threatening Rose.

"They'll kill us," he said, trying to sit up.

"They're gone." A gentle hand stroked his hairline. "The men are gone. They can't hurt you."

Something pressed against his stomach. He reached down and touched the dog again. He jerked his hand away.

"It's okay," she said. "Oscar will protect you. I will protect you."

For some reason her words felt like a hypnotic suggestion. He sighed and drifted into the darkness.

"You should go home," a male voice said.

"I'm not leaving him again," a woman responded.

Noah recognized Rose's determined voice.

"Not leaving him?" the man said. "You don't even know him."

"I know enough."

Noah forced his eyes open. Surrounded by white, it took him a minute to figure out where he was. Surely not heaven. Such a place did not exist for men like Noah.

No, he was in the hospital. Rose stood at the foot of his bed with her arms crossed in a defiant stance. She reminded him of a mama bear guarding its cub.

"Good, he's awake. You can go now."

Noah glanced left at the source of the comment, and saw Detective Harper.

"You're awake." Rose came to Noah's side and touched his hand. "How do you feel?"

"Like I was hit by a Humvee going sixty."

"I need to ask you some questions, Mr. Greene," the detective said.

"Give the guy a chance to wake up, T.J." Rose

poured water from a small pitcher. "Are you thirsty?" she asked Noah.

Noah nodded. He didn't mind being taken care of by this woman, even though in his experience people who helped Noah usually had an ulterior motive.

Except Thomas.

"How did I end up here?" Noah said.

"Two men attacked you at the motel last night. Do you remember?" the detective pressed.

"A little. They wanted to know about Thomas."

A doctor joined them. "Mr. Greene, I'm Dr. Motts. How are you feeling this morning?"

"Morning?"

"Yes, you slept through the night, probably due to the benzodiazepine."

"The what?"

"A sedative. It will have to work its way through your system. We've wrapped your bruised ribs and the CT scan showed a concussion, but your vitals are good. I'll sign the paperwork to have you released shortly."

"Thanks." And go where? Noah couldn't go back to the motel.

The doctor left the room.

"Noah?"

He looked at Rose.

"Why not come back to the ranch and—"

"I'll keep him in protective custody at the station," the detective said.

"In a jail cell," she said, her voice flat.

"The cots are comfortable."

"That works," Noah said.

"The man has PTSD," Rose argued with the detective, ignoring Noah's comment. "The last place he needs to be is behind bars."

"I'll be fine," Noah tried again.

"You'd be better at the ranch," she said to Noah. "I've called my brother to pick us up." She offered a smile as she touched his hand.

The warmth shot clear up his arm to his chest. What was happening to him?

"Do your folks know about this plan?" the detective said.

"Yes, they had a family meeting, and everyone agreed we should help an army veteran until he gets his bearings."

"This could be dangerous, Rose," the detective said.

"We've faced danger before, and we do fine. Beau will be here shortly."

The detective shook his head and left the room.

"He's right," Noah said. "It's not smart to have me around."

"Stop talking like that. You're the victim, and the Rogers family is here to help."

On cue, a tall, dark-haired man entered the room.

"Noah, this is my brother, Beau. Beau, meet Noah."

They shook hands, Beau holding on a second longer than necessary, as if assessing what kind of threat he was bringing back to the family ranch.

"Veteran, huh?" Beau said.

"Yes, sir."

"You're welcome to stay at the ranch if you agree to our rules—be honest, be kind and work hard."

"You realize you're saying this to a man who is being released from the hospital," Rose said.

"After you recover," Beau corrected.

"It would be an honor to do all three of those things in exchange for temporary lodging, sir."

"You don't need to call me sir. Makes me feel old."

"If the saddle fits," Rose teased.

Beau narrowed his eyes at her.

Noah enjoyed watching the banter between siblings. It reminded him of how the guys in his unit would rib each other.

They spent a few minutes going over the ranch's schedule, expectations of employees and guests, and sharing a bit of its history. Apparently Rose's father gave up a fast-moving career as an investment banker to buy the guest ranch and start a new life in Montana. He and Rose's mother felt it a healthier environment for raising children.

Parents who sacrificed for their children was a foreign concept to Noah, since he felt like an afterthought growing up. He sensed his mother felt obligated to have children and did her duty, but neither parent cared much about Noah's needs, didn't realize he was being bullied in school, nor did they seem to care that an undiagnosed learning disability was holding him back.

Noah was on his own from an early age, and got out of his tumultuous household as quickly as he could when he'd enlisted at seventeen.

A nurse entered the room. "You're all set to go."

Noah sat up and took a deep breath; the room seemed to spin a little.

"I'll help Mr. Greene get dressed and an orderly will bring him to the front entrance," the nurse said.

"Maybe I should wait," Rose hesitated.

Beau shot her a curious look. Noah would be curious too if his sister had become attached to a stranger in less than twenty-four hours.

"Go with your brother," Noah said.

"C'mon, Rose," Beau said. "You can fill me in on the details about what happened yesterday."

"Okay, see you in a bit," Rose said with that charming smile of hers, and left his room.

Whenever she walked away it felt like she took the light with her, only to be replaced by a dark cloud of doom.

Noah was losing it.

"Let's get you dressed." The nurse helped him put on his jeans and cotton shirt.

He moved slowly, sore pretty much everywhere thanks to the beating he took at the motel, plus his head was still a little foggy from the drug.

"I can take it from here," he said, grabbing his jacket.

"The orderly will be by soon."

Noah slipped one arm into his jacket, then the other. Leaning against the bed, he forced himself to stay alert and not give in to the exhaustion. He needed time to sleep off the sedative, time to get his head clear.

Rose's family's ranch seemed like a good place to recover and strategize, but he'd leave as soon as he was steady on his feet. Noah didn't want to bring more danger to the woman and family who had offered him temporary refuge.

A young man in his twenties pushed a wheel-chair into the doorway.

"Are you ready to break out of this place?" the kid said, opening the footrests.

With a nod, Noah shuffled to the wheelchair and collapsed, feeling way past his age of thirty-four. The orderly wheeled him down the hall into the elevator.

As the doors closed, two men joined them, one in his thirties and an older man in his fifties with gray hair. The older guy hit the roof button.

The hair on the back of Noah's neck bristled. No, he was overreacting, being paranoid.

"Sorry, were you going down?" the older guy said.

"We'll get there eventually," the kid said.

Since the two men stood behind Noah, he couldn't assess their demeanor to determine if they posed a true threat.

"So, what's on the roof?" the orderly asked.

"Meeting a friend," one of the men answered.

The elevator doors opened to the rooftop. "Let's go, kid."

"What? No, I'm taking the patient to the lobby."

"We're all getting out here."

Noah's instincts were right on. "Leave the kid out of this."

Instead, the younger guy grabbed the orderly and shoved him out of the elevator. The gray-haired man guided Noah's wheelchair onto the roof. The doors shut with a deafening thud.

These weren't the same men who'd assaulted Noah at the motel, so they weren't working for Stratosphere. Were they foreign agents trying to find Thomas for the code he'd supposedly promised them to breach US government servers?

An accusation the Feds shared with Noah back in Virginia, but one Noah did not believe.

"Let go!" the orderly said, trying to pull away. The younger man slugged him in the gut and the kid fell to his knees.

"Leave him alone," Noah said.

The gray-haired guy stood in front of Noah. "We'll let him go, after you cooperate."

Noah fisted his hands, but couldn't muster the strength to even get out of his wheelchair to fight back.

Helpless, vulnerable.

You're worthless, soldier.

Burning regret of the past rushed through his body. His mind sinking into that profound, dark place again.

"Where's Thomas?" the gray-haired guy demanded.

"I don't know."

The younger man pulled the orderly to his feet and led him to the edge of the rooftop.

"What are you doing?" the kid protested.

With an arm around the kid's neck, the younger assailant threatened to toss the orderly over the railing.

"That's enough!" the older guy ordered his partner.

Instead, the younger one started to hoist the orderly over the edge.

Noah's heart raced and his adrenaline spiked. Another innocent. Dead because of him. Like the mother and child, a little dark-haired boy.

"Stop! I don't want to die!"

I don't want to die. I don't want to die.

Through a blur of memory Noah saw Thomas,

his best friend, walking through fire and extending his hand to Noah.

"Thomas," Noah said.

"Where? Where is he?" the gray-haired guy demanded.

Noah shook his head, realizing the image of his friend had been a hopeful mirage.

The gray-haired guy gripped Noah's shoulders. "Where is Thomas!"

"Help, help me!" the kid wailed.

And disappeared over the rooftop.

FOUR

"Something's wrong," Rose said, leaning against her brother's truck.

"Stop fretting and tell me more about Noah Greene so I can assess what we're dealing with."

"He's a veteran with PTSD from Virginia."

"And…?"

She glanced into the hospital lobby through the glass doors. "It's taking too long."

"What is with you? You've known this guy less than a day and you're acting like he's family."

"He's in trouble, Beau."

"I'm sorry about that, but I'm not thrilled we're bringing more trouble back to the ranch."

"Then why are you here?"

"You know Dad. Always helping the underdog."

"You make that sound like a bad thing."

"I have every right to be cautious here, Rosie. You're getting attached to a stranger awfully quickly."

"Noah is vulnerable and has no one to turn to. I know that feeling."

"You do? How?"

"Never mind, he needs our help."

"I get it, I do. But it's stuff like this that makes us worry about you."

"Why, because I helped a man? You know how ridiculous that sounds?"

He sighed. "It's like you're trying to prove something."

"You're overanalyzing this."

"You've gotta admit you've attached yourself to him like barnacles on a boat and you haven't a clue who he is, or who's after him."

"Great, another lecture. I'm going to see what's taking so long." She headed for the sliding doors.

His words stung, and not only because it was another big-brother lecture. They stung because once again someone in her family was not trusting her ability to make good decisions. His words made her second-guess herself. Had she grown inappropriately attached to Noah?

The resounding answer in her heart came quickly: *no.*

Noah needed help and she and Oscar were able to give him support. She'd continue to offer Noah a grounding presence as long as he needed it.

She headed into the hospital, scolding herself for the slip about feeling alone. She didn't want her family to know about her emotional trials dating back to high school. It would do no good to admit to them what had happened because they would only circle the wagons and try to bring her back into the fold.

Besides, she was beyond the pain, the trauma. Wasn't she?

She approached the receptionist. "I'm waiting for Noah Greene. The orderly was supposed to bring him down?"

"I'll call up to the nurses' station."

As she made the call, Rose scanned the area, hoping to see Noah being wheeled toward her from the elevator.

"I'm calling about Noah Greene. Was he picked up by the orderly? Oh, okay, thanks." She hung up and looked at Rose. "Picked him up ten minutes ago."

"Thanks." Rose went to the door and motioned her brother inside. "Something's wrong."

"Get the on-duty psych up to the roof ASAP," a security officer said into his radio as he passed Rose and Beau. "Possible suicide attempt."

She and her brother shared a look, then quickened their pace. Rose bypassed the elevator and rushed to the stairs. In a blur, she took them two at a time, her big brother right behind her. They got to the rooftop door, and she reached out to open it.

Beau put his hand over hers. "Take a breath."

She nodded. *Please, God, don't let him give up.*

Beau swung open the door.

They took a few steps onto the roof when the elevator doors opened. A doctor and two nurses joined them.

"Are you family?" a nurse asked.

Rose nodded, not knowing how to explain her presence. Beau didn't correct her.

The five of them scanned the immediate area. The only sound, the frantic beating of her heart.

Followed by the sound of whimpering. Her gut clenched. She knew that sound, the sound of panic, fear, utter devastation. And she knew the feeling, how it nearly destroyed her if not for her faith.

As the five of them rushed to the edge of the roof, the doctor put out her hand to indicate she would lead the effort to save Noah's life.

The doctor leaned over the edge. "Hello, I'm Dr. Narra."

"They tried to kill me!"

Rose exhaled with relief.

It was not Noah's voice. He hadn't jumped or fallen...or been pushed by brutal men.

The nurses approached the edge, and so did Rose. A young man in his early twenties was trembling on a rooftop, one story below.

"Where's Noah?" Rose blurted out.

"Ma'am, please step back," Dr. Narra said.

"He went with them. They were going to kill me," the kid said.

"To be clear, you weren't trying to harm yourself?" Dr. Narra said.

"No! I'm getting married next month."

"Okay, hang tight while I figure out a safe way

to get you down from there." Dr. Narra motioned to the nurses. "Talk to him to keep him calm."

"Yes, Doctor."

Dr. Narra made a call. "This is Dr. Narra at Saint Michael's Medical Center. I need an emergency rescue from a third-floor rooftop, and police. One of our orderlies has been assaulted."

"My friend," Rose said. "He was a patient, and they took him."

"We believe a patient may have been taken against his will... Thank you." Dr. Narra ended the call. "They're on the way."

Rose didn't know what to do. All that she'd gone through to help Noah in the last twenty-four hours, and it was for nothing? She'd failed to help him after all.

Helplessness, defeat hovered low. No, she wouldn't give up. "May I ask him a question about my friend?" Rose said.

"If you don't upset him," Dr. Narra said.

Rose went to the edge. "Hi, I'm Rose. Was Noah okay when they left?"

"Yeah. They wanted to know about some guy named Thomas."

"Noah's friend."

"Mr. Greene said he'd take them to his friend if they got me help."

Rose straightened and looked at her brother. "Noah doesn't know where Thomas is."

"That's what he told you."

"Beau, he really doesn't. And when they figure that out…"

"Don't go there, Rosie." He led her back toward the elevator. "He's a veteran. He knows how to defend himself."

"He's injured, he's got PTSD and he's recovering from being sedated. Beau, we have to find him."

"Step it up," the gray-haired guy ordered.

"Going as fast I can, considering I've been beaten and drugged," Noah said.

He'd offered to take them to Thomas in order to lure them away from the hospital and innocent people like the orderly, whom Noah thought had been dropped to his death, until the kid cried out in pain.

Not dead. Noah wasn't responsible for another innocent person's death.

"This is taking too long," the younger guy said, and brushed past Noah on the trail. As the guy jogged ahead, he slipped on the wet trail and went down to one knee. He glanced to his right and the steep drop below.

"You go over and I'm not coming after you," the gray-haired guy said.

Noah had purposely chosen a steep trail he remembered from yesterday in the hopes of shaking these guys. Whom was he kidding? He was struggling to stay upright, much less be able to neutralize two healthy, determined men.

You did not think this through, soldier.

His goal had been to prevent innocent people from being hurt.

Like Rose.

"How much farther?" the gray-haired guy said.

Noah hesitated. "It's probably a five-hour hike on a good day, and I'm still recovering from your people's assault at the motel."

"Not my guys."

Interesting. There were two different teams on the hunt: the pair from yesterday sent by Stratosphere and these guys, who were potentially sent by a foreign country to find Thomas and retrieve the software allowing them to access US government systems.

"Russia or China?" Noah said.

"What?" the gray-haired guy said.

"Who sent you to find Thomas for his software?"

"Would you believe, the US government?"

"No, I wouldn't believe that."

Because federal officers wouldn't kidnap a suspect or threaten to kill an innocent orderly. Then again, Noah had agreed to go with them, and the orderly was alive.

The gray-haired guy was messing with his

head. Noah couldn't afford to be manipulated in his current state. He glanced briefly at the river below. Would he survive the fall if he chose that way to escape?

"What's your cut?" the younger man said over his shoulder.

Noah thought he was talking to his partner at first, then the gray-haired guy poked Noah's shoulder. "He's talking to you."

"My cut of what?"

"Selling out your country," the younger guy said.

Now what should he say? If he denied being Thomas's partner, they might figure out he didn't know where to find his friend.

"How much are you getting?" the younger one pushed.

"Enough," Noah said.

"I want a number." The younger one stopped and blocked Noah. "I want to know the price for betraying your country."

A chill ran down Noah's spine. What if these guys were actually working for the government, either an overzealous team, or a covert one given permission to cross the line to find Thomas and bring him back for crimes against the state?

The younger guy's eye twitched. "You think your friend will share his bounty with us in exchange for your life?"

"Knock it off, Smitty," the gray-haired man said.

Smitty's eye twitched again, then he turned and continued the trek. "Know what I think? I think you guys will give us whatever we want in exchange for leaving your families and friends alone."

The image of Rose's heart-shaped face and green eyes flashed across his mind. If these guys had intel, they could find anyone, retrace Noah's steps and…

No, he'd blocked access to his cell phone using software he'd designed in his spare time. He hadn't called anyone, hadn't…

Rose. He'd accidentally called her from the motel yesterday.

His eyes darted over the edge again, then back to Smitty.

Noah had to get away, had to tell someone about the danger, warn Rose.

The sound of a barking dog echoed across the canyon below.

"Great, now we've gotta deal with wolves?" Smitty said.

"Wolves howl, they don't bark," the gray-haired guy said. "They probably sent search-and-rescue."

Or was it Rose, hoping her dog could find Noah like he had before?

They approached a sharp turn, heading left, away from the steep drop.

Noah had to do something, and fast. A distraction.

More muted barking echoed through the canyon.

He took a deep breath. Readied himself.

As they made the turn, he glanced down the mountainside and pretended to see his friend. "Thomas? Thomas, get outta here!"

His captors took the bait and glanced below.

With whatever strength he had, Noah charged the younger guy from behind. The momentum took them both over the edge of the trail and down the mountainside.

As Noah slid down the mountain, he tried protecting his head to avoid further brain trauma. Suddenly he hit the rocky shore, his head spinning, stars exploding across his vision.

Through the haze, and the sound of rushing water, he heard a man curse. The guy named Smitty grabbed Noah by the jacket collar and pointed a gun in his face. "Give me a reason not to kill you right now."

Noah closed his eyes. At least he'd die in a beautiful place.

Suddenly he was released.

"What—uh," Smitty grunted.

Noah struggled to focus. He saw what he thought was Thomas in hand-to-hand combat with Smitty. It couldn't be Thomas, they weren't in Afghanistan, his friend wasn't fighting an insurgent to save Noah's life.

"Thomas." Noah collapsed on his back, staring up at the trees bordering the river.

Moments later his view was blocked by Thomas's concerned frown. "Are you hurt? Did you break anything?"

The sound of barking dogs grew louder. Thomas cast a worried glance over his shoulder. "You didn't see me, buddy. Please, just go home, go back to Virginia."

And then he was gone.

"Thomas," Noah groaned, and passed out.

Rose wished they would have let her bring Oscar along on the search. He might have found Noah by now. Since the coltriever hadn't been properly qualified, and wasn't an official member of the team, the SAR leader wouldn't approve the last-minute canine addition.

It had taken a lot of persuading to convince the detective to let her come along. With support from Simon, T.J. finally agreed not to send her away when she showed up to join the search.

They'd been following the phone signal until a half an hour ago when they'd lost it, probably due to spotty reception.

Rose was surprised when Beau joined the search, and appreciated the gesture at first. Then she wondered if he was tagging along to protect Rose from herself. Her big brother wasn't an SAR regular, but periodically offered help tracking someone or bringing an injured hiker down from the mountains.

"Last known location is about—"

"Over there, look!" Simon interrupted T.J.

Rose glanced to where he was pointing.

Two bodies lay on the riverbank.

"That brown jacket, it's Noah," she said, looking for a way to cross.

"Rosie, stop," Beau ordered.

"Base, we've spotted two bodies by the Grant River, about two miles south of Spring Falls. Send emergency, over," T.J. said into his radio. "Get your sister out of there," he said to Beau.

Rose was already crossing the river by carefully stepping on a bank of rocks that bridged to the other side.

"Rosie!" Beau said.

"Don't disrupt my concentration." One foot in front of the other. Well-placed steps would get her safely to the other side.

To Noah.

Please, God, let him be alive.

Beau's words haunted her. Was she too attached to Noah, a stranger? Was she trying to prove something?

Her motivation didn't matter. A man needed her, a fragile veteran.

She hesitated for a second, inhaling the fresh mountain air.

"What's wrong?" Beau said. He was right behind her.

"Clearing my focus." She glanced around, and realized a few more team members, including T.J., were following her route to the other side, while the two K-9 handlers stayed on shore.

"I'm surprised you followed me," she said.

"Gotta look out for my baby sister," Beau said.

"Right." She refocused on crossing the river, shutting out the seeds of resentment from his comment. "Be careful, the rocks are slippery," she warned.

"I know that," he said.

A few seconds later, she heard a splash and glanced over her shoulder. Beau was waist-deep in water.

"I was hot anyway," he said, wading to the other side.

At this rate he'd get there before Rose, which was potentially a good thing. He could assess the bodies, determine if Noah was okay and if the other guy was still a threat.

Give me strength, Lord.

Although she didn't know Noah well, they'd made a connection, probably due to the traumatic manner in which they'd met. Or was it something else? Had God brought them together for a special purpose?

A few more steps…

Give me courage.

When she stepped onto the rocky shore, Beau was beside the stranger feeling for a pulse.

"He's alive," Beau said. "Beat up pretty bad."

Sure, Noah's kidnapper was alive, but what about Noah?

Simon joined her and they approached Noah, who lay on his back, his eyes partially open. Was he…?

Suddenly, he blinked. She bit back a gasp and kneeled beside him on the cool rocks.

"Thomas," he said, blinking again.

"No, it's Rose. Remain still until we can assess your injuries."

"Rose?" He turned his head to look at her.

His blue eyes watered. With pain? Or relief to see her?

"Yes, it's me." She placed her hand over his.

He turned his palm up and clasped her fingers. "You're here."

"I'm here."

"Where's Thomas?"

She glanced at Simon, then back at Noah. "He's not here. We're in Montana, remember?"

"Your dog…found me?"

"No, I had to leave Oscar at home. He's not qualified for SAR and the team thought he might go willy-nilly and distract the other dogs." Once again she was rambling, but the words kept coming out because she was so relieved.

"Willy-nilly?" Noah repeated.

"Yeah, crazy, all over the place, wonky, off-the-wall. You know how Oscar is."

"Yeah."

Simon kneeled on the other side of him. "Sir, I have medical training. Can you tell me where you're injured?"

"My head."

"How about your neck, back, anything else?"

"My arm." He nodded toward his left arm. "I fell from up there."

That's when Rose noticed blood seeping through the jacket. She redirected her attention to Noah's face. He studied her, making her slightly uncomfortable.

"Okay, Rose, we'll take it from here," T.J. said, approaching.

Noah clung to her hand, so she didn't move.

"The other guy…" Noah said.

"Seriously injured and unconscious." T.J. kneeled beside Noah. "Did you do that? Did you assault him?"

Rose held her breath.

"No, sir. I can barely stand."

"Could have sustained injuries from the fall," Simon offered.

Another team member tended to the unconscious man.

"Who is he?" T.J. pressed.

"One of the guys that took me from the hospital."

"What did they want?" T.J. said.

"To find Thomas."

"And you were leading them to Thomas's location?"

"No, sir. I don't know where he is." He turned away, as if ashamed.

Perhaps ashamed by his confusion when he regained consciousness and thought Rose was Thomas.

"Then why bring the men out here?" the detective asked.

"To get them away from…" He looked directly at Rose. "From innocents."

"What can you tell me about them?" T.J. pressed.

Rose wished he'd leave Noah alone, but understood his need to work this case.

"They claimed to be with the US government."

"And they want to find Thomas because…?"

Noah shook his head.

"I could charge you for obstructing an investigation."

"C'mon, T.J.," Rose said. "He's wounded."

T.J. ignored Rose and addressed Noah. "The sooner you shed light on any of this, the better equipped I'll be to protect you and our community."

"I understand, sir. But I don't have clear answers for you, and I'm a little dizzy."

T.J. nodded. "We'll talk more later."

"Thank you, sir."

Rose nodded at T.J. as he stood. He went to check on the other man.

She felt Noah squeeze her hand and she looked at him.

"Thank you," he said.

"T.J.'s just doing his job."

"I meant, for finding me."

"You're welcome."

"But don't do it again. Stay away from me, Rose. Far away."

The rest of the day had been fraught with tension and frustration. Sure, Rose had heard Noah's request, but she couldn't bring herself to comply.

He was so alone, and needed an ally. He was pushing her away, a behavior she'd perfected in her own life. Deep down, a part of her wished someone would have pushed their way through her carefully erected walls and offered help, compassion.

When they had brought Noah down from the mountains, he refused to be admitted to the hospital since the bad guys had found him there, and he didn't want to risk putting others in danger again.

Bad guys. Who were they? She wished he would confide in her. Since they'd returned to town, he'd barely looked at her, much less spoken to her. It was almost as if he was ashamed.

None of this was his fault. He'd done nothing wrong.

Not easy to believe when you've been a victim of brutality. She sighed and continued to pet Oscar as they sat in her truck outside the police station.

Brutality. Or in her case, assault that she'd convinced herself she'd recovered from. Being around Noah had somehow triggered the hidden pain.

But this wasn't about Rose and her mistakes.

It was about a traumatized soldier who needed help.

Helping others seemed to ease one's own pain. She'd learned that when she offered to bring Oscar into the nursing home in Seattle for pet visits. Rose always felt better, her trauma smaller, after seeing the elderly residents' eyes light up when Oscar approached, tail wagging, offering unconditional love to each and every person.

She hadn't had much time for volunteer activities when she'd returned to Montana. She dedicated herself to helping her family grieve the loss of her sister and assisting with getting the guest ranch up and running again. Once they started welcoming guests, Rose wasn't quite ready to leave, but didn't want to slide back into old habits, unhealthy behaviors of letting her family think they could manage her life better than she could. There were moments when her family still treated her like the baby of the family, like a silly, irresponsible kid.

Rose decided to rent an apartment in town to set her boundaries because Mom, Dad and Beau didn't believe her smart or clever enough to make good choices.

Was helping a man in danger a good choice? It definitely had been the right choice in the moment, and she hoped on some level it might finally make her parents proud: their daughter had saved a man's life. She'd also hoped they were proud of her for starting her own business as a dog trainer and property manager when folks were out of town. In a matter of weeks, she had multiple inquiries from locals needing help with their pets and their homes. With God's help, she'd grown her business into a self-sustaining enterprise, one she could close whenever she felt it was time to move on.

She picked up burgers and fries for both Noah and the deputy who was on duty tonight, hoping to convince the deputy to let her see Noah. She wanted him to know she hadn't and wouldn't abandon him.

Even though he'd ordered her to stay away.

As her mind was still processing that proclamation, her gut held firm: *he needs you, like you needed someone in your darkest days.*

Dark days that haunted her every now and then. If she'd learned anything from her struggles with depression, it was that being alone made things worse. She'd forced herself out and joined a self-help group that discussed sadness and depression in a safe space. In time, between the group meetings and volunteer visits with the elderly, she began to feel much better.

Being alone with your pain was not the answer.

Too bad Noah didn't realize that. He seemed the type to embrace his isolation, to have surrendered to it. She could not live that way.

She eyed the police station and took a deep breath. If T.J. was inside, she knew she'd get an earful, another lecture from another person in her life who saw her as a flighty woman needing help, needing direction.

Well, she had direction all right. She would help Noah one more time by letting him know he was not alone, and he wouldn't be as long as he was in Boulder Creek. Her determination to offer her assistance felt good, like she was on the right course.

The Lord had opened this door and she was walking through.

"I'll be back, Oscar." She grabbed the white bags of food and headed for the entrance to the building.

"I hope this doesn't backfire on me," she said. Would Noah refuse to see her, be angry and say hurtful things? She would brace herself for the possibility. All she could control was her actions, not how he responded to them.

Besides, she suspected his words would be born of fear: fear of Rose being pulled into this violence and getting hurt.

She hit the buzzer, glanced at the camera and held up the food bags. "Food for you and Noah Greene." She flashed a hopeful smile.

A moment later the door clicked open, and she went inside. She ambled down the hallway past a dark office and conference room, to a lit office on the left.

"Hello?" She stepped into the office.

It was empty. Papers were scattered across a desk, and the swivel chair was pushed back.

It was like someone had left in a hurry.

She placed the bags on the desk. "Hello?"

The muted sound of Oscar barking from her truck shot chills down her spine.

"Nooo!" a man cried.

She snapped her head toward the source of the sound: the doorway leading to lockup. She crossed the room and cracked it open.

"Don't kill me! Please don't kill me!" Noah pleaded.

FIVE

Heart pounding, Rose shut the door and stepped back. She wanted to run but didn't want to abandon Noah.

She darted behind a file cabinet, out of view of the door. Took a few deep breaths and processed who could get here the quickest to help Noah.

She instinctively called T.J.

Moments later, his ringtone echoed from across the room.

T.J.'s phone was here, in this room. Which meant...

Someone had hurt or killed T.J. in their effort to terrorize and kidnap Noah?

She called Emergency.

"9-1-1, what is your emergency?"

"T.J.—Detective Harper, sheriff's office... someone's here. They're trying to kill Noah," she whispered.

"Ma'am, what's your name?"

"Rose. I'm at the station. Someone's trying to kill—"

The door to lockup swung open. Rose stopped talking, ended the emergency call and prayed.

Seconds ticked by like hours. She heard the sound of paper rustling.

"Rose, Rose, where are you?"

She stood and saw T.J. analyzing the bag of takeout. "You're okay?"

"Sure, what did you…what are you doing back there?"

"I heard shouting, Noah pleading for his life."

"He's having another episode."

She approached his desk. More muted cries of an emotionally tortured man echoed through the door. She must have looked horrified because he said, "I called someone to give him a sedative."

"I can help."

"No, Rose. Let a professional handle it."

"When is the doctor coming?"

"Not sure."

Another angst-ridden cry made them both look at the door.

"You seriously think you can help?" T.J. said.

"I know Oscar can. Be right back." She went to her truck and got the dog. "Noah needs you, buddy."

She and Oscar entered the station and T.J. led them back to Noah's cell. His breathing was quick and shallow, and his back was pressed against the wall.

"Let us in," she said.

T.J. opened the cell door. "Go on, boy," she said to Oscar.

The dog slowly approached Noah and stopped about a foot away. Whining, he looked back at Rose. She joined him in the cell, kneeling beside Noah.

"Right here, Oscar." She gently tapped Noah's thigh.

The dog edged closer.

"Hey, Noah. Look who came to see you. Remember Oscar?"

His glassy eyes were unfocused, his breathing still labored.

"You're safe now. Oscar's here. I'm here. Take a breath with me in—" she took a breath "—and out. Slow and steady."

Her words didn't seem to pierce through his trauma.

She tapped Noah's thigh again, and Oscar placed his chin there. She took Noah's hand and held it against the dog's side. "Feel his breath, Noah? Feel how slow it is?"

Not that Oscar's breath was super slow, but it was slower than Noah's, who she suspected was having some kind of an anxiety attack.

His fingers twitched against her dog's fur. Something was getting through.

"Slow and steady," she said. "Inhale on the count of four."

He blinked and looked at her. She nodded encouragement. "Count to four, inhale." She illustrated. "Hold for four. Exhale on four. Inhale."

She counted to four, held her breath and nodded four times. Then blew out her breath.

Noah seemed to follow her lead. A buzzer echoed from the other room.

"Must be the doctor," T.J. said, and left them alone.

Rose continued the breathing exercise with Noah. After doing this a few times, his pained expression softened, the rise and fall of his chest slowed, and his eyes seemed more focused.

On her.

It felt a little disconcerting.

"Box?" he said.

"Yes, the box breathing technique. You know it?"

He nodded, then glanced at Oscar, who looked up at him with soulful eyes. "You saved me again, buddy. You and your master."

Someone cleared his throat. T.J. entered the cell with a male doctor.

"How are you feeling, Mr. Greene?" the doctor, in his late sixties, said.

"Better."

"Would you like something to help you sleep?"

"No thank you, sir."

The doctor glanced at T.J. "Why don't you two wait outside so I can examine Mr. Greene."

Rose squeezed Noah's hand and offered a comforting nod.

"Can he stay?" Noah nodded at Oscar.

"It's okay with me," Rose said, standing.

"Sure, that's fine," the doctor agreed.

Rose and T.J. left the cell area. She absently went to the desk and dug into the white to-go bag. Pulled out a burger and realized she didn't have an appetite.

"That was… What you did in there was amazing," T.J. said.

"Thanks."

"To think I'd let you in tonight for the free food, and to give you a lecture about staying clear of this."

"Do we even know what 'this' is?"

"No, but we've got a lead on the guys who tried to kill Greene the first time."

"I don't think they wanted to kill him, but they definitely wanted him for something."

"Something related to his friend Thomas?"

"That's my guess. What about the guy from the river?" she asked.

"Hasn't regained consciousness yet."

The door to the cell area opened and the doctor joined them. "He refuses medication. He seems lucid, so I can't force the issue." He glanced at Rose. "Whatever you did made a big impact, plus the presence of the dog seems to be helping. He shared his medical history. It's PTSD, probably triggered by violence or location. Isn't there anywhere he can stay other than a jail cell?"

"It's a matter of safety," T.J. said. "Both his and the rest of the community's."

"He'll be safe at the ranch," Rose offered.

"Rose." He shook his head.

She shoved back the shame triggered by his tone. "I've already cleared it with the family."

"It would be better for his recovery to be some-place—" the doctor hesitated "—peaceful."

"I supposed a hospital isn't exactly peaceful," T.J. said.

"Or a jail cell," Rose said.

The doctor nodded his agreement.

"I'll send a deputy to stay at the ranch for protection," T.J. said. "We need to get him there without being noticed."

"I can make that happen," Rose said.

They sneaked Noah into the back seat of the doctor's car and arranged a rendezvous point with Beau, who was waiting with a horse trailer. They figured the trailer would serve as a Trojan horse of sorts.

Rose drove her truck to the meetup point, and once the detective was satisfied they hadn't been followed, they transferred Noah into the horse trailer.

She'd been unsure why she felt compelled to stick with Noah every step of the way until this very moment, when Beau was about to shut the trailer doors.

Noah's expression hardened. He glanced around the dark trailer with wide blue eyes.

She stepped inside the trailer and knelt beside Noah. "What is it?"

He shook his head. "I'm fine."

A practiced response she knew well.

"Could you get Oscar?" She tossed Beau keys to her truck. "He and I will ride with Noah to the ranch."

With a nod, Beau disappeared from view. She heard him speaking in low tones to Detective Harper, the two of them probably questioning the wisdom of this plan, but her main focus was on Noah.

He suddenly looked at her. "Why are you doing this?"

"Sorry, I know you asked me to stay away, but this seems like the best strategy to keep you safe for the time being."

"I asked you to stay away to protect you, but you keep finding me, helping me."

She sat cross-legged next to him. "I may not have fought in a war like you have, but I've experienced my share of trauma. I'm in a good place to help you, so that's what I'll do."

"Did someone help you?"

"God."

"Not…friends?"

She shook her head. "They didn't know what had happened. I didn't tell anyone."

Oscar jumped into the trailer and started sniffing around. The smells were fascinating for the dog.

Beau poked his head inside. "Ready?"

"Yep," she said.

"I'll pull up to the barn and escort him to the cabin."

"Sounds good."

She suspected Beau uttered the pointed comment to make it clear he expected Rose to keep her distance from Noah once they reached the ranch.

"Drive slowly, please," she said.

"Yes, ma'am," Beau said and shut the door.

Oscar continued to sniff every corner of the trailer. With a jerk, they started moving and Oscar crouched, looking at Rose.

"Right here," she said.

Oscar approached and nuzzled Noah, who automatically touched Oscar's fur. Noah's fear of dogs was easing, which could be a sign he was on the path of healing from his trauma.

She didn't push him to talk as they made their way out of town toward the ranch. Her goal in riding with him was to ease his burden, help him feel calm, and she sensed he wasn't comfortable chatting and sharing.

With a gentle hand, he stroked Oscar's fur. "They say it helps to talk about it to other people," he said suddenly.

She glanced at him. His eyes were closed, as he continued his rhythmic stroke of her dog.

"What, the traumatic event?" she said.

"Yes, ma'am."

"Have you talked to anyone?"

"No," he said.

They hit a slight bump in the road, and she lurched sideways into Noah's shoulder. "Sorry."

"No need to apologize."

They continued a few more minutes in silence and she felt like she was helping him simply by being here.

"Airplane friends," he said.

"Excuse me?"

"You know, that thing where strangers share intimate details of their lives to a fellow passenger because they'll never see them again." He nodded, waiting.

She inhaled a quick breath, not sure how much to tell him, if anything.

"Okay, I'll start so you'll know what you're getting into by letting me stay at your ranch," he said. "In Afghanistan, my unit was doing a sweep of a village. I was off to the side, talking to a local. A man came out of nowhere with a semiautomatic rifle. I… I had no choice."

"That was self-defense."

He shook his head and closed his eyes. "He was using his wife and little boy as a shield, figuring we wouldn't shoot them."

"Oh, Noah."

"My team… They froze. I had to save their lives."

"I am so sorry."

"Now you see why your God would want nothing to do with me."

"God forgives, Noah."

"I can never be forgiven for that."

She took his hand and said a silent prayer for God to ease his burden.

"I can't even imagine how horrible war is."

"Pretty horrible. I wasn't sure why I even existed. After that I ran straight into danger without hesitation almost as if…"

"You wanted to die?"

"Yes, ma'am."

"I think I understand."

He glanced at her. "You do, don't you?"

"Yes. But my burden doesn't even compare to what you've been through."

"Everything is relative," he said. "Pain is pain."

"I suppose you're right. Well, I'm the youngest of the Rogers clan. My big brother and sister were always so confident and independent. They made my parents proud, Beau with his football wins and Cassie with her grades and extracurricular activities. Then there was Rosie, the baby of the family who seemed to need help all the time. They treated me like I couldn't do things on my own. Looking back, I'm not sure that was completely true, but I guess I can see their perspective, since I was the youngest." She hesitated. "You don't want to hear this."

"Yes, I do. It's distracting me from the anxiety of being caged and transported like an animal."

"Oh, I'm sorry. Maybe this was a bad idea."

"No, I'm fine. Please continue."

"In high school I was desperate to prove myself to them like my older brother and sister had repeatedly done, so I joined the science club. Our project made the state finals. My folks were so impressed." She remembered the smiles on their faces, and the joy it brought her. "They called me Dr. Rose because I talked about becoming a veterinarian when I grew up. Anyway, something happened on the Science Fair trip. A boy touched me, inappropriately. I was so naive back then. I didn't know what was happening or why."

"Aw, Rose, I'm sorry. Did you tell your parents?"

She shook her head. "I felt too ashamed."

"It wasn't your fault."

"I know that now, but when it happened…" She sighed. "I couldn't tell them. It would have only confirmed their opinion that I wasn't able to take care of myself and make good decisions. They would have closed ranks even more to keep me safe."

"Did you tell anyone, any adults?"

"No, but I told my best friend, who was also

on the trip. She discouraged me from reporting it to the school, and then, get this, she ended up dating the jerk when we came back home. In one day, I had lost my innocence and my best friend. I kind of withdrew after that. My parents sensed something was off, so I started pretending, acting like everything was okay. I moved away at twenty so I wouldn't have to pretend around them anymore."

"Did it help?"

"A little. Then it happened again."

"What?"

"A few years later a guy at work backed me into a corner and I froze." She shuddered. "That incident triggered guilt and shame. It made me wonder if I was doing something that was attracting this kind of behavior."

"No, Rose, this is not about you. It's about jerks who think they're entitled to whatever they want when they want it."

"Anyway, trust is not something I do, especially where men are concerned. Dogs, on the other hand, are the best."

She glanced up and caught his gaze. The empathy she saw there made her look away. She didn't want his pity, didn't want him to feel sorry for her. After the office incident, she'd decided never to be perceived as weak again.

"I'm okay," she said.

"How did you become 'okay'?"

"I found a job at an animal clinic in Seattle owned by a female vet. Then I enrolled in self-defense classes to become a strong, independent woman. I hate being weak."

A slight chuckle escaped his lips.

"What?" she challenged.

"You've rescued me from gunmen, kidnappers and even from myself. You, Rose Rogers, are anything but weak."

The trailer started to slow down. "We can't be there yet," she said and stood to get away from his compassion, his praise.

It was a good break in the conversation, an important break. She could barely believe she'd exposed that much of herself to a stranger. The knot in her chest she usually needed prayer and meditation to uncoil seemed to have eased. Maybe he was right about the whole airplane-confession thing. Besides, it probably made him feel better about accepting her help if he could return the favor by listening to her story.

The trailer came to a complete stop, and she peered out the top window. Couldn't see much of anything.

Noah took her hand and coaxed her to sit next to him, this time on the other side, away from the trailer door.

She heard the truck door open and shut. "What's the problem?" Beau said.

* * *

Man, Noah wished he wasn't still aching from the fall down the mountain, and wasn't a bit blurry from the traumatic episodes he'd endured the past few hours. He wanted to be at the top of his game so he could protect Rose if those trailer doors opened to an armed gunman.

As he clung to her hand, he realized it had been a long time since he'd had a physical connection to another person, especially a woman. He'd come home from war carrying the weight of guilt and self-loathing on his back, which basically destroyed his relationship with his girlfriend, and any other relationships thereafter. It's like he wore a flashing sign that read *Stay away.*

Yet the warmth of this remarkable woman's hand eased up his arm to fill his chest.

He gave it a squeeze and let go, needing to focus on the potential danger outside the trailer. He hoped her brother was able to defend himself. Noah hated the thought of Beau being hurt, or anyone in her family, for that matter, because of Noah's presence.

He needed to heal and get away from the ranch as soon as he was able.

As they sat quietly, he felt Rose's hand on his shoulder, grounding him, depending on him.

Like his men had back in Afghanistan. Only, now he didn't have a weapon with which to defend himself. Then again, maybe that was a good thing because he wouldn't want to shoot and kill someone in front of Rose, exposing what a brutal man he was.

Oscar suddenly sat up and barked. Noah stiffened, not so much because of his fear of dogs, but because Oscar had announced their presence.

"Quiet," Rose said softly and ordered him to lie down.

Noah listened more intently to what was happening outside.

"...yeah, well, you don't know Oscar," Beau said. "He likes it back there. C'mon, I'll help you change that tire."

Noah sat back down. "He's helping someone with a flat."

She nodded and rubbed Oscar's ears.

She didn't look worried exactly, but something bothered her.

"I'm sure your brother can handle it," he said in a low tone.

"Right, he can help a stranded motorist, but I can't help a wounded veteran. You'd think since he's such an altruistic guy that he would understand my actions."

"It's not quite the same thing."

"Are you siding with my brother?" She narrowed her eyes.

"I'm trying to understand everyone's perspective. But I do agree that he should be able to understand your motivation. I doubt he would have abandoned me in the mountains."

"See, that's what I said."

"That must be a family trait, helping people."

She nodded. "It is."

Noah only hoped the stranded motorist Beau was helping wasn't working for the other side.

The flat tire incident had been, in fact, just that—Rose's brother helping out a fellow motorist.

A few hours later Noah found himself surrounded by the Rogers family at a long, wooden dining table. They wouldn't have it any other way. Apparently Beau's plan to escort Noah directly to his cabin didn't sit well with Lacey and Bill Rogers, Rose's parents, and instead they requested Noah join them for dinner before settling in for the night.

The Rogers family chatted away about their business, their lives and the neighbors. They occasionally asked Noah a question, and he'd respond politely with short answers. He noticed the family didn't push him to reveal more than he was comfortable sharing. He figured Rose had clued them in that Noah wasn't a big talker.

He'd confessed his sin to Rose in the horse trailer, for her sake more than his. He figured telling her his brutal truth would both expose who he was, encouraging her to keep distance, and give her permission to share her secrets that he sensed were still festering, even though she claimed to be *okay*.

He took a bite of barbecue pork, savoring the flavor of garlic, onion, pepper and other spices. Noah couldn't remember the last time he'd had a home-cooked meal, and had never eaten at a table like this, surrounded by family: Rose's parents, Lacey and Bill, and Rose's niece, Miri, and her father, Jacob Rush. Rose explained that Jacob had been engaged to Rose's sister, but her sister abandoned Jacob and came back to Montana... pregnant. Jacob had no idea he was a father until Rose's sister died and the family contacted him about his child. Talk about trauma.

Noah had initially declined the family's dinner invite. When Rose explained that the family had waited for Noah to commence the family's private meal—they usually ate with guests and wranglers—he felt like he should join the group. Just for this one meal. After dinner he'd explain that in the future he'd eat in his cabin, staying out of sight to prevent his pursuers from finding him, and the others, at the ranch.

From finding Noah before he located Thomas.

Noah was more convinced than ever that he was close to finding his friend. After all, if it weren't for Thomas, Noah might be dead right now, shot by the assailant claiming to be working for the US government.

"Potatoes?"

Noah glanced across the table at Jacob, who passed him the bowl.

"Sure, thanks."

"Afghanistan, huh?"

"Yeah."

Jacob offered what could only be described as a sympathetic nod.

"Careful, he's a head shrinker," Beau said.

"Shut up, Beau," Rose said.

"Make me."

"Don't tempt me."

"I'm sorry, Noah," Lacey said. "They're only like this when we have company."

"Ah, they're trying to show off," Bill added.

"Ha, ha," Rose countered, then looked at Beau. "You wouldn't be poking at Jacob if Brianna was here. You actually have manners when a doctor's in the house."

"Doctor?" Noah said.

"My wife is a neuroscientist," Jacob said, then smiled. "*My wife.* I'm still getting used to saying that. We're newlyweds."

"She's my new mommy." The little girl named Miri climbed off the bench and came over to Noah's side. She blinked her big green eyes at him, and held up an owl made from a pine cone. "Mommy knows a lot about owls. Hoot-hoot."

The sweet child's face, her innocence and pureness, caused a knot of emotion to form in his throat.

"Hoot-hoot," she said and waited, like she was expecting something in return.

"Hoot-hoot," Noah replied.

"He likes you." She held the owl up to Noah's cheek and made a kissing sound.

His eyes burned with unshed tears. What was happening to him?

His gaze followed Miri as she went to sit next to her dad. All eyes were on the delicious food in front of them at the Rogerses' table. It was like they sensed Noah's turmoil and were offering him space to breathe.

He took a few slow, deep breaths to calm the heady emotions bubbling up inside. Being around the warmth of this family and the innocence of a child reminded him of all that he would never have. He didn't think it bothered him before tonight, before being embraced by such an authentic, loving family.

A wave of sadness washed over him, or was it grief? Was he already grieving something he hadn't even known he ached for until tonight?

"We're glad you could join us for dinner, Noah," Bill said. "We usually eat with the guests and rest of the staff, so we understand if you'd prefer to dine privately in your cabin during your stay with us. It can get pretty rowdy in here with all those folks telling tales about their wilderness adventures."

"That would probably be best, thank you, sir."

"We can have a breakfast basket dropped off at your cabin tomorrow morning around eight, but for lunch feel free to stop by the kitchen and grab a sandwich," Lacey said. "We're all pretty busy even with limited guests on-site, so you won't mind taking care of yourself?"

"No, ma'am."

"Oh, and all our wranglers know that you're our—" Lacey made quotes with her fingers "—'special' guest. That means you've got added protection. We'll all be on the lookout for strange or unwanted visitors."

"I can't thank you enough for being so generous and risking your welfare for a stranger."

"We're experts at offering a safe refuge," Rose piped up.

"My wife was the first to hide out here for her own safety," Jacob clarified.

"Not the first," Beau said softly.

"Right, sorry. You guys helped a young woman years ago," Jacob said.

"Harriet," Beau said.

The room fell silent. Noah was curious about who Harriet was and why her name seemed to be the one thing that could shut down Rose's brother.

"You know how to ride?" Jacob asked Noah.

"No, sir."

"We could teach you while you're here."

"Thank you, sir, but I need to keep a low profile. And hopefully find my friend."

"Maybe later, after things are resolved," Rose offered.

Later? There would be no *later*. Noah suspected this wasn't going to end well for him or Thomas. The sooner Rose understood that, the sooner she could make better choices in regard to her own safety.

"So, you think your friend is camping in the mountains?" Rose's dad asked.

"Or he has a cabin up there."

"Rugged wilderness north of Columbia Falls, although there are a few cabins scattered here and there."

"And a multimillion-dollar resort," Beau said.

"A resort?" Noah said.

"Don't get him started," Rose said.

"I'm justified to want to keep the wilderness pure, Rose. Not polluted by capitalism."

"I don't disagree. Sorry, I was teasing. Probably not the right subject."

"Sorry? You actually said you're sorry?" Beau leaned back and pretended a look of shock.

"Don't make me take back my apology."

Beau smiled and went back to eating his sandwich.

As a few minutes passed, Noah realized how good it felt to be around people who cared so much about each other that they could disagree without permanent damage. Noah didn't have a lot of experience with those kinds of relationships outside of his unit.

The doorbell rang and Rose stood. "I'll get it."

As she crossed the room, the rest of the family continued their lighthearted banter, discussing ranch operations and activities for the guests.

Noah embraced the rhythmic sound of their discussion, spoken in pleasant tones that created a calm, relaxing atmosphere.

"Hang on, stop," Rose said.

Noah glanced toward the front door. Detective Harper stepped around her and headed into the great room.

"Hello, Detective," Lacey greeted. "Join us for some barbecue pork?"

"Thank you, Lacey, but not tonight." Harper pulled cuffs off his belt and approached Noah.

Noah's heart sank.

"Noah Greene, stand up and put your hands behind your back."

SIX

"T.J.—"

"Detective Harper," the detective cut Rose off.

"Detective Harper, what's going on?" Lacey said.

"I'm here to make sure this man doesn't pose a threat to your family, and he doesn't disappear again."

"A threat?" Beau said.

The room fell silent.

Jacob stood and took his little girl's hand. "Let's get the dessert, sweetie." Jacob led her away, casting a sympathetic glance at Rose as he passed.

Once he and Miri were out of sight, Detective Harper pulled Noah's hands behind his back and cuffed him. "Let's wait in another room, away from the family." Noah awkwardly stood.

"Wait for what?" Rose asked.

Rose's dad stood. "Detective, please tell us what's going on."

"Federal agents are on the way to question Mr. Greene about suspected crimes against the US government. I'd like to detain him in the den until they arrive."

"Of course," Dad said.

Detective Harper led Noah away. Rose groaned inwardly. There was no way Noah would turn on his country. She started after them.

"Rosie," her dad said.

She glanced at her family's worried expressions.

"God put Noah in our lives for a reason," Rose said.

"Don't be naive, Rose," Beau countered.

That one word triggered a burst of anger in her heart. Naive Rose who couldn't protect herself, who trusted her best friend. Naive Rose who didn't realize despicable people could be standing right in front of you and you wouldn't even know it until you'd been badly hurt by their betrayal.

Noah was not despicable. She knew it in her heart.

She turned away from her family, not responding to Beau's harsh words for fear she'd say something hurtful. Oscar trotted alongside her as she headed for the den. She hesitated outside the closed door.

"Please, Lord, give me patience," she whispered.

She took a deep breath, knocked and opened the door. Oscar rushed to Noah, who sat in a leather chair, staring blankly at the floor. Detective Harper, who loomed over Noah, snapped around and glared at Rose.

"Go away, Rose."

"Are you arresting him?"

"That's not up to me."

"Is he being questioned about a crime within your jurisdiction?"

"Not yet."

"Keeping him secure for federal agents is one thing but intimidating him is inappropriate and you know it."

His phone buzzed with a call. "Harper." He brushed past her out of the room. Rose closed the door.

She pulled a chair beside Noah and sat down. Oscar nudged Noah, trying to get Noah to pet him, but Noah's hands were secured behind his back.

"He's right," Noah said. "You shouldn't be here."

She tipped his face to look at her. "Tell me what's going on."

"You heard him. Feds want to question me about crimes against the US government." He looked away.

"We both know that's not true."

"What do you want from me?"

"The truth."

"I don't want to involve you any more than you already are."

She placed her palm against his cheek. "I'm already involved, and you need my help."

Noah released a heavy sigh. "The Feds questioned me back in Virginia about Thomas. They suspected someone at Stratosphere of selling a special code to foreign enemies, they think Russians, to access US government servers. Thomas was their top suspect. He hadn't been at work for a few days, and wasn't returning my calls, so I went to check on him. His apartment was trashed. I searched for clues and was assaulted but got away. I sensed someone following me for days after that. I thought Thomas might be in danger and I had to help him somehow."

"You think he's in Montana because…?"

"When I was recovering from military trauma, having a particularly bad day, he'd tell me stories about a place where you could escape in nature, forget the past and not worry about the future. 'Montana's the place, buddy,' he'd say, and described it in such detail that it distracted me from the oppressive darkness. So, here I am, looking for Thomas, a needle in a haystack."

"To warn him about the trouble he's in?"

"Yes, and to help him."

"But if he's involved with—"

"He's not. He'd never turn on his country. We all shed too much of our own blood to do that."

Rose nodded. She hoped Noah was right, and that he wasn't in for a major disappointment if his friend turned out to be a criminal.

"A part of me thought…" Noah's voice trailed off.

"What?"

"That he was dead."

"Did something change your mind?"

He glanced into her eyes with a mixture of regret and desperation, like he needed to tell her something, but feared doing so.

"Rose—"

The door opened and Detective Harper entered. "Agents will be here in the morning. I'm moving you to a cabin far away from the house." He looked at Rose. "No visitors."

"What about Oscar?" Rose said.

"I'd rather not risk the dog getting hurt. Let's go." Harper grabbed Noah's arm.

"Surely he doesn't need to be cuffed," Rose protested.

"I'll uncuff him when we get to the cabin. C'mon, I've got two deputies waiting outside."

Noah glanced over his shoulder at Rose. "Thank you. For everything."

Which sounded oddly like *goodbye*.

The next morning Rose was up way too early, mostly because she hadn't slept. Neither had Oscar. The coltriever paced the spare room where he and Rose spent the night, almost as if he was waiting for Noah to walk through the door.

It was unusual how attached Oscar had become to Noah.

How attached Rose had become.

She wouldn't let Noah leave the ranch without

an official goodbye from both Rose and Oscar. She made her way to the kitchen to prepare breakfast for Noah and the deputies who were guarding him. What did they do, sleep in their patrol cars? That would have surely announced Noah's location to the bad guys.

No, T.J., or rather "Detective Harper" as he'd clarified last night, probably had them park in the empty barn and stay in the cabin with Noah. Detective Harper wasn't so angry about the situation that he'd intentionally put a bull's-eye on Noah's back by leaving cruisers in plain view.

Rose entered the kitchen, which smelled of fresh coffee and baked goods. She glanced in the oven at two trays of cinnamon rolls.

"You're up early," her mom said, joining her.

"Apparently not the first one up."

"Dad and Beau had some work to do on the fence before they tended to guests, so Dad popped a few things in the oven. Such a sweet man."

Her mom poured two cups of coffee and passed one to Rose. She sipped the warm brew. "Wow, that's good. You changed the blend."

Mom leaned across the breakfast bar. "It's a mushroom blend. Shh, don't tell your father or brother."

"Mushrooms?" Rose eyed the coffee.

"Adaptogens to keep us healthy and maintain homeostasis."

"I have no idea what that means, but okay."

Mom reached out and rubbed Rose's arm. "It was so nice to have you stay with us last night. I wish you'd move back in."

"I know, Mom. I know."

"But you like being on your own."

"I do." She sipped her coffee.

"I get it. We were probably overprotective of you growing up."

Rose glanced up.

"It's because we love you so much and didn't want to see you hurt. I'm sorry if you felt smothered."

"Thanks. It's all good."

They shared a moment and Rose thought Mom might cry.

"Hey, what is it?" she asked Mom.

"It's a parent thing. You never stop worrying, no matter how old your kids are."

"You're questioning my decision to help Noah?"

"No, we're all meant to help one another. It's not that."

"What, then?"

"Beau says you've grown very attached to Noah."

"Right, Beau, the guy who has pushed every female prospect away since Harriet left. He's in no position to judge."

"You can understand why he's concerned, especially after losing Cassie."

"I get it, Mom. But what you guys have to accept is I'm tougher than I look, and smarter, too." She kissed her mother's cheek.

When she leaned back, Mom teared up again. "Mom?"

Mom waved her off. "Sorry, didn't sleep much."

"Join the club."

"Age is my excuse. What's yours?"

"Worried about Noah."

Mom shot her a concerned look, then sighed. "He does seem like a nice fellow."

"I was going to bring Noah and the deputies breakfast."

On cue, the timer beeped. "I'll help you pack some goodies," Mom said. "Should we scramble eggs and microwave some bacon?"

"Sure, that would be great. I guess enough for four? In case Detective Harper also stayed over."

"T.J. did not look happy last night." Mom pulled cinnamon rolls out of the oven and glanced at Rose. "Is it truly over between you two?"

"It is. I won't be Cassie's seconds." Rose sighed. "I'm sorry, that sounded—"

"Honest. It's okay. Come on, let's make eggs."

Twenty minutes later Rose and Oscar were headed to the cabin with freshly baked rolls, bacon and eggs, and coffee. The bonding time with Mom in the kitchen had been a true blessing. They'd even shared a laugh when Oscar used his "puppy dog" eyes to persuade Mom to share a slice of bacon with him.

As she crossed the property to the Glacier Cabin, Rose suddenly wondered if it might be too early for the breakfast delivery. Someone should be awake, especially if the goal was to keep an eye on Noah 24-7 until federal agents arrived.

She stepped onto the wooden porch and placed the basket of food and thermos of coffee on the bench. Should she knock? Would that awaken Noah from a deep and much-needed sleep?

"Can I help you?"

She turned to a deputy standing behind her. His badge read *Jackson*.

"I'm dropping off breakfast and coffee for you guys," she said.

"I think he's still asleep. Rough night."

"What do you mean?"

"Night terrors, I guess. Pretty bad."

"I should have left Oscar with him." The dog wagged his tail at the sound of his name.

"He must have seen some bad stuff overseas."

She remembered the story Noah had shared with her.

"He finally quieted down around three a.m."

"How about some coffee, bacon and eggs, and cinnamon rolls?" She figured she could stall for a while, perhaps until Noah awoke.

"Sure, that'd be great."

She poured coffee into a disposable cup. As

she handed it to him, she noticed T.J.'s cruiser coming up the road. Perhaps an offer of cinnamon rolls would discourage T.J. from launching into a lecture at the very sight of her.

He got out of his car and Oscar rushed to him, wanting extra attention. Detective Harper petted the dog as he approached.

"Good morning, Detective," she welcomed. "How about some coffee?"

"Thanks, that'd be great."

She poured another cup from the thermos.

"Still asleep?" he asked Deputy Jackson.

"Yes, sir. Had a rough night."

Rose didn't offer her opinion about not allowing Oscar to stay. No reason to irritate Detective Harper first thing in the morning. Especially if she wanted to say goodbye to Noah before the Feds whisked him away from the ranch.

"Agents are meeting me at the station at eleven. I can take over," the detective said.

Deputy Jackson glanced longingly at the basket of food.

"Go ahead," Detective Harper said. "Help yourself to breakfast first."

The deputy's eyes lit up and he went to grab a pre-plated breakfast out of the basket.

"Rose, was there something else?" Detective Harper said.

"Oh, I'm being dismissed?"

"I figured you had a full day ahead of you."

She did have a full schedule between training class in town for three dogs and checking on the Brewer Ranch.

"I wanted to say goodbye to Noah before he disappeared," she said.

"We'll swing by the house on our way out."

"Thanks."

She stepped off the porch and headed for the house. Even though the detective seemed distant, she believed he'd keep his word. At least she hoped he would.

After everything she and Noah had been through in the past two days, she needed to say a proper goodbye, and wish him well.

Oscar was trotting happily beside her and suddenly stopped. His ears pricked.

"Oscar, sit," she ordered, both to figure out what he sensed and also to stop him from taking off on her again. Maybe if she respected his instincts he'd be more likely to respect her commands?

He went very still and cocked his head.

She kneeled beside him. "What is it, buddy?"

He'd been exposed to the wildlife on the property surrounding the ranch long enough not to get excited by a random deer.

As she petted the dog, she also listened beyond the typical sounds of morning.

Then she heard it. A distant groan. Was it an injured animal?

No, it sounded like a man. Had one of their guests been hurt on an early morning walk?

"Okay, buddy."

She released his collar and motioned with her hand. "Go!"

Oscar sprinted toward the forest and disappeared into the thick mass of trees that bordered the property. Rose took off after him, not scolding him or demanding his return. Instead, she respected the dog's instincts.

Mom must have seen her racing after the dog, because she called out from the house. "What's wrong?"

"Get Dad! I think someone's hurt!"

Rose weaved her way through the forest. "Oscar, speak!" she called, needing to know his location.

When he didn't respond, she stopped running, calmed her frantic heartbeat and listened.

Silence, then the sound of Oscar whining, followed by a short bark.

She made her way through the mass of trees and bushes, hoping the guest hadn't been seriously injured because Rose didn't have a first aid kit and wasn't sure how far away Dad and Beau were.

Rose burst through the foliage to the riverbank and stopped short. Oscar released a playful bark. She turned and saw her dog lying beside Noah, who sat inches from the water.

"What are you doing out here?" she said.

He glanced up. "I wanted to see the water one last time."

She approached and crouched beside him. "How did you escape the cabin?"

"No escape. I opened the door and no one was there. So, I went for a walk."

"Deputy Jackson was supposed to keep watch to make sure no one threatened you."

"You mean, to make sure I didn't take off again."

"In any case, they'll be looking for you."

"I know. I've resigned myself to my fate. But I needed…to take a piece of this with me." He reached out and she automatically placed her hand in his. "And this, this memory."

She had imagined saying goodbye, but not like this, like he'd disappear forever, almost as if he'd never existed.

They'd never met.

She wanted to help him replace his old, horrific memories with new, peaceful ones to see him through his future trials.

"Close your eyes," she said.

He shot her a look.

"Trust me. This will help you remember even better."

He did as she requested.

"Focus on the sounds of nature," she said. "Let the scent of pine and earth permeate your skin. Take a few deep breaths in…and out."

She wanted to anchor the moment in his mind so he could remember it whenever he felt off-kilter or on the verge of panic. The grounding energy of nature always calmed Rose's anxiety.

She inhaled with him, and exhaled.

It was an exercise she'd use to help her feel the peace of God when stress and the frantic pace of city life became overwhelming.

They breathed in and out a few times. Then he opened his eyes.

"Amazing," he said.

Their eyes locked. Yes, she knew without a doubt he'd remember this moment.

So would Rose. She'd remember the peaceful, beautiful respite of grace she shared with a stranger who didn't feel like a stranger at all.

"I could sit here for hours," he said.

"Tempting as that is, I actually have work to do."

"Dog work?"

"Yeah, I have a training class in town, then I'll head over to the Brewer Ranch. I'm keeping an eye on the place while the owners are away. Bring in the mail, water plants, that sort of thing." She kept talking to ground herself in reality, remind herself that she had a life filled with responsibilities, a life without Noah.

"Where are the owners?"

"Out of town, looking at places to retire. They

can't manage the ranch. It was once a working ranch, but not anymore."

He nodded, glanced at the river and inhaled deeply. "I will miss this."

And she would miss him.

She stood, needing to break the intimate moment before she got lost in his vibrant blue eyes. Federal agents would whisk him out of town. This was the only time she and Noah would have together.

It was, in a word, lovely. The more she basked in the moment, the more it would hurt when he left.

"Let's get back before Detective Harper sends a search party," Rose said.

"You're upset with me."

"No, not at all. I don't want you to get in more trouble because you went on a nature walk."

"Rosie! Rosie, where are you?" her dad called.

"Over here!" Rose answered.

Noah stood and took her hand. "I... I will never forget this." He hesitated. "Or you."

Her dad and brother burst onto the riverbank, and he released her. Another few seconds alone and she thought he might have kissed her.

"We're A-OK," Rose said to Dad and Beau. "Noah wanted to see the river one more time."

"We thought someone was hurt," Beau said.

She looked at Noah. "I heard moaning."

"When I sat down. My back's still sore from the fall yesterday."

"Probably not good to sit on the hard ground with a back injury," Dad said. "Can you walk?"

"Yes, sir."

Beau motioned them out of the forest onto the ranch property. Dad accompanied Noah and Rose to the cabin, while Beau headed to the barn for chores.

As they approached the cabin, Detective Harper caught sight of them, and his jaw practically dropped. He said something to Deputy Jackson, then marched across the property toward Rose, Noah and Dad.

"I should have handcuffed you to the bed," the detective said to Noah.

"Hold on, Detective," Dad said. "He's returning to your custody of his own free will. He didn't try to flee the property."

Rose felt proud that her dad was standing up for Noah. And relieved. She was too tired to get into another fight with Detective Harper.

"Jackson, take him to my cruiser," Detective Harper ordered.

The deputy jogged over. Rose gave Noah's hand a squeeze.

Remember. Remember our moment.

He turned and was led away by the deputy.

"He never should have left the cabin," the detective said.

"He wanted some peace by the river before he was locked up by federal agents," Rose said.

Detective Harper was about to counter with an argument when Dad interjected, "This place, our glorious part of the country, fills a person's heart and soul with peace. If you'd been here, and he'd asked your permission, would you have denied him a last moment in nature? T.J., he fought for our country."

"I'm just doing my job, Bill." He looked at Rose. "Have you said your goodbyes?"

"Yes."

"Good. Bill, thanks again for letting us keep him here." With a nod, Detective Harper walked away.

"He's right, you know," Dad said. "He is just doing his job."

"Okay, but does he have to be so…angry about it?"

Dad put his arm around her as they watched the detective and deputy lead Noah to the deputy's unmarked sedan. Dark clouds in the distance matched her mood, and signaled the coming of rain.

"There's nothing worse than not being able to protect the people you love," Dad said.

"T.J. doesn't love me," she said.

"Well, he cares about you, and our entire family, and the whole town of Boulder Creek for that matter. Can you imagine how hard it is to protect an entire town of people you care about?"

"I see your point."

As Detective Harper pulled away, Rose and Noah made eye contact. She shared a warm smile, so that would be his last memory of her.

"I've got a good feeling about Noah," Dad said. "I think he'll be fine."

At least the detective cuffed Noah's hands in front this time, a more comfortable position. Due to the lack of sleep and soothing movement of the car, Noah found himself drifting into a semiconscious state. He remembered the sound of the river, the smell of pine trees and the brilliance of Rose's emerald eyes.

The feel of her hand on his cheek, grounding him, causing a surge of calm to flood his system. How could that be from only knowing her two days? She'd probably say it was God's plan to bring them together.

He took a slow breath, letting himself drift even further to feel the warmth of Rose's hand, the softness of Oscar's fur.

The peace that filled his heart.

"Meet me at the station, over," the detective said.

His voice startled Noah out of his half asleep, half awake state.

"10-4," Jackson responded on the radio.

Detective Harper put the radio in its cradle and glanced into the rearview mirror. "If it were up to me, I'd put you on a plane to Virginia and get you out of my county."

"Right, remove the threat as quickly as possible."

"You're admitting you're a threat?"

"Not intentionally. But yes, somehow I've drawn enemy fire, which puts the people around me in danger."

"Somehow," Harper said, his voice flat.

"I know you have a hard time believing this, but all I wanted was to find Thomas. I'm not involved in espionage or anything against the country I almost gave up my life to defend."

"A part of me would like to believe that."

"And the other part?"

"Needs to keep the Rogers family safe. They've been through enough death and danger in the past few years. They're good people, really good people."

"I agree. I would never do anything to intentionally cause them harm, especially since Rose saved my life." He hesitated. "More than once."

"Her sister died in a car accident a few years ago, did she tell you that?"

"She did."

"That's probably why she's so intent on helping you, because no one helped her sister. If they'd only seen the car..." His voice trailed off.

"Accidents are tragic."

"Which is why I don't want more tragedy to befall this family, you got me?"

"Understood."

Noah glanced out the window at the darkening sky. It seemed like the Rogers family had experienced their share of trauma, and then some. Noah felt relieved he was being taken away for good, that his presence wouldn't bring more danger to a family that was still trying to mend from death and grief.

He drifted back into a semiconscious state. In the past, the images that filled his brain were ones of blood and death, destruction of human life. The sound of his friends fighting for survival. Their cries of panic and pain would echo in his mind, sounding so real he thought he was back in battle.

Not today. Today the images were of the trees and water, of a pleasant family dinner in the Rogerses' home. Siblings teasing and challenging each other, round and curious eyes of a little girl, and the wagging of a dog's tail.

The smile on Rose's face the last time he saw her through the window of the cruiser as they drove away from the ranch.

Better. These were much better images to carry around as opposed to the gruesome images of war. What purpose did it serve to torture himself with what he'd done as a soldier? None.

He snapped awake with a start. He wasn't sure

how long he'd been out, but the road they were on was bordered by a lake on one side and thick trees on the other.

"Base, this is Detective Harper. I need assistance at—"

Something hit them from behind.

The car jerked forward and skidded on the damp pavement.

Harper gripped the steering wheel with both hands, trying to regain control of the vehicle. "Hold on!"

He spun the wheel away from a cluster of trees.

They were slammed again, forcing them off the road toward the water.

The front grille hit the lake with a thud.

"Emergency! Officer needs assistance at Juniper Lake." Harper whipped open his door and exited before the front of the car was completely submerged.

Noah pounded on the window with his fists, but there was no way out.

Then the door opened, and Harper helped him out, both men submerged up to their chests. They struggled to get to shore, Harper's hand firmly gripping Noah's upper arm.

Pfft. Pfft.

"Uhh!" Harper gasped, released Noah and fell into the water.

With cuffed hands, Noah grabbed the detective and pulled him toward a cluster of trees bordering the riverbank. The detective groaned, triggering Noah's traumatic memories. Noah struggled to shut them down and stay present.

Once he safely got the detective onshore, Noah checked him for injury. That's when he spotted blood seeping down the detective's arm.

"I need to get a look at your arm." He tried pulling off the detective's jacket, but the cuffs made it difficult.

"Pocket, keys in my left pocket."

Noah hesitated.

"Do it," Harper ordered.

Noah retrieved the keys and removed his handcuffs. He read surrender on Harper's face, like he thought the minute Noah uncuffed himself he'd disappear, taking the detective's reputation and career with him.

"It's not bad," Noah said. "More than a flesh wound, but not serious."

"You practice medicine on the side?"

"I've seen my share of gunshot wounds."

Noah shucked his jacket and shirt, used his cotton undershirt to wrap the detective's wound. As Noah put his clothes back on, he scanned the area for better cover. He eyed the perfect spot, helped Harper to his feet and led him into the thick forest.

"Give it up, Greene!" a man shouted.

Noah and the detective scrambled beneath a fallen tree that made for perfect natural cover.

"We've gotta talk to you!"

Talk? After shooting a cop? They were way beyond talking.

"How's the detective? Still alive?"

Noah calmed his breathing. Focused on what he needed to do to save the detective's life. It felt like they were in a foxhole waiting for the enemy to pass.

Or discover their location.

Noah couldn't risk it, couldn't risk their killing the detective. His best move was to distract them, draw them away. After all, they didn't want a local cop; they wanted Noah.

"They're after me, not you," Noah whispered to the detective.

The detective shook his head. "You're in my custody. I'm supposed to protect you."

"You did. Now I'm protecting you." Noah took off, breaking through the trees, intent on leading them away from the detective.

"There!"

Pfft. Pfft.

So much for wanting Noah alive. He zigzagged his way to the water's edge and dived into the lake.

Stroke, stroke, stroke, breathe.

He noticed an island in the distance when the car drifted into the water. If only he could make it there, he could find temporary safety and give Harper time to call for help.

Exhausted from a poor night's sleep, he appreciated the cold temperature of the water to keep him sharp. He hoped the gunmen saw him swimming across the lake and realizing they couldn't follow him would give up the hunt for today.

The hum of a motor echoed across the lake. A boat? How did they find a boat so quickly?

Didn't matter. He had to stay focused.

Stroke, stroke, stroke, breathe.

The humming grew louder…

Louder.

Until it sounded like it was right on top of him.

SEVEN

Rose hovered outside the ER hoping to see T.J. to make sure he was okay and find out what had happened.

She was finishing up her puppy training class at the local pet store when an employee raced in and announced that Detective Harper had been attacked by a suspect he was transporting to jail.

Which Rose knew was not true.

Apparently some relative of a relative was driving by and saw Detective Harper being loaded into an ambulance. That sighting, plus frantic texting by someone from the hospital, ignited rumors that accused Noah of assaulting the detective.

"Are you waiting for someone?" a nurse asked as she approached Rose in the hallway.

"T.J. Harper. I'm…" She hesitated. Calling herself his ex-girlfriend wouldn't give her access. "He's a friend of the family. Is he okay?"

"I can't share a patient's information, I'm sorry."

Rose nodded and paced the hallway. She texted Beau that T.J. was in the hospital and Noah had gone missing. Beau already knew. Yes, word traveled like wildfire in a tight-knit community like Boulder Creek.

The door opened to the ER and a doctor exited. Rose glanced both ways and sneaked inside. There was only one area sectioned off by a curtain. She approached and listened for sounds of a nurse tending to a patient. When Rose heard nothing, she slowly pulled the curtain back. T.J.'s arm was bandaged, and he had an IV in his other arm, draped over his forehead.

"T.J.?" she said.

He removed his arm. "Rose? What are you doing here?"

"I heard you were brought to the hospital. Are you okay?"

"I've been better."

"The gossip mill is buzzing. People are saying Noah assaulted you and escaped."

T.J. shook his head and pinned her with dark brown eyes. "He... He saved my life, Rose. He found me cover and took off."

"I'm not surprised."

"He dived into the lake to lure them away from me. Why would he do that?"

"He doesn't want to put more innocent people in danger."

"The Feds have requested a search. If you decide to go with them, please be careful, okay?

These guys are brutal and if they figure out Noah's got a connection to you, they might use that as leverage against him."

Two hours later Rose was part of the SAR team assigned to the mountainous area northwest of Juniper Lake. Simon, SAR team leader, chose the coordinates based on a report from residents who lived in the area and helped Noah out of the lake in their speedboat. The locals took him back to their cabin, where they gave him dry clothes and something to eat. He said he wanted to thank them by restocking their wood.

He went outside and never returned.

Which could mean he'd been found by the guys trailing him, or he'd fled his rescuers' cabin so as not to put them at risk.

Simon coordinated the mission and invited Rose to join the group. She'd helped Noah before, and Simon figured if they found Noah in a vulnerable state it would be good to have Rose on the team.

A friendly face.

Today's team consisted of Simon, Federal Agent Doug Hart, in his fifties with graying hair, an off-duty sheriff's deputy they called Scooter and two female SAR K-9 team members in their forties. The plan was that the SAR team would find Noah and notify base. Law enforcement officers were ready and waiting for the call to assist.

Assist with what? T.J. had made it clear to his colleagues that Noah had saved his life, so why were they all still treating Noah like a threat?

"Remind me, how do you know the suspect?" Agent Hart asked Rose.

"My dog and I found him."

"Found him?"

"Yes, he was being hunted by two creeps from the center where he works."

"*Hunted.* Interesting word choice."

"They were armed. He was not. He was also suffering from a PTSD episode, which put him at a disadvantage."

"And you rescued him?"

"I protected him until it was safe to regroup with SAR."

"Awfully brave of you."

"Thanks."

"Must be a Montana thing, putting yourself in the line of fire to help a stranger."

"It's a Christian thing, you know, helping your fellow man?"

He didn't respond for a few seconds, then said, "You developed a connection to him from that one incident?"

"It was more than one incident." Rose explained how Oscar found him behind the motel after Noah had been assaulted, how they'd rescued him after he'd been taken from the hospital and then how she'd smuggled him onto her family's ranch.

"And you didn't know him before that first time you found him?" the agent said, skepticism in his voice.

"No, sir."

Rose suspected what the agent was thinking, that Rose had gone way beyond helping a stranger when she'd brought Noah to her family's ranch. But then, sometimes doing the right thing came with risks.

"If it were up to me, I wouldn't have included civilians on this search," Agent Hart said.

"Noah is not dangerous. Besides, SAR is made up of civilians. You'll find him quicker with the K-9 SAR team."

On cue, Simon's Labrador mix stopped and sniffed the air. The dog took off, racing into the wilderness and out of sight.

"What's that about?" Hart said.

"He caught scent," Rose explained.

They were close, close to finding Noah, rescuing him from this nightmare. Only to be tossed into another one? Accused of helping his friend break federal laws and betraying his country?

The group picked up the pace. The dog returned to Simon, tugged on the toggle at his belt and took off again. The other two K-9 dogs chased after him.

Rose said a silent prayer that Noah was not seriously injured and would be able to help authorities in order to gain his freedom.

Erase any suspicion they had about him being a criminal.

They caught up to the dogs, and the handlers gave them the order to step back. Simon knelt and picked something up off the ground.

A jacket she didn't recognize; one Noah might have borrowed from the people who'd rescued him from the lake? It was chilly out, so why would he take it off?

"We'll need to release a new description of clothing," Agent Hart said to the deputy. "Find out what kind of shirt the Good Samaritan gave him. Why would Greene shuck the jacket? It's not exactly warm out here."

Rose shared a look with Simon.

"What?" Agent Hart said.

"If he had an episode, he might get confused and do things that don't make sense," Rose offered.

"Or he's trying to throw us off his scent," Agent Hart said.

"Hey, Noah isn't the bad guy here," Rose countered.

"It's convenient that the detective was shot, but Mr. Greene was able to swim away to freedom."

"Freedom? He's being hunted, again."

"We've got the jacket," Simon said. "Let's keep going and see if they pick up anything else."

Rose kept to herself after that, but was glad she'd decided to be a part of this search considering Agent Hart's attitude about Noah. With Simon, the off-duty deputy and two other SAR members on the team, Rose felt confident the agent wouldn't overstep.

She hoped, anyway.

As they continued, Rose decided it best not to engage with the federal agent.

He'd obviously made up his mind about Noah. There was nothing more for her to say.

The dogs caught scent again and rushed off. The handlers increased their pace, with Agent Hart and the deputy right behind them. Rose brought up the rear, a mix of hope and dread in her heart. Hope that the dogs had found Noah; dread that the federal agent would arrest him on the spot.

As the group turned a corner up ahead, someone grabbed Rose and yanked her into the woods. She started to scream—

"Shh, it's Noah."

Rose looked into his blue eyes and nodded that he could remove his hand.

"You're okay," she said.

And then she hugged him.

* * *

He broke the embrace and pressed his finger to her lips. He led them deeper into the woods, hoping this was the right move, but then he had no choice.

He had to get her away from the gray-haired guy.

Noah found shelter earlier beneath a fallen tree and waited until he could distract the dogs with another article of clothing. Thankfully he'd remembered reading a wilderness survival article about masking your scent with a plant called Stinky Bob. He'd spotted it the other day when the men took him from the hospital and that observation had saved him today. The dogs caught scent of his clothes, but were thrown off by the plant residue rubbed on his skin.

As he led Rose away from the search team, he realized she came willingly, without question.

She trusted him that much.

They ascended a trail up a hill and back down to the other side where they waded through a creek. Another strategy to help mask their scent.

Rose didn't question him, or balk at getting her clothes wet.

Finally, when he thought they were safe, he paused and turned to her. "I'm sorry about all this."

"What's going on?"

"That man with the gray hair—"

"Agent Hart?"

"He was one of the guys from the hospital yesterday. He said he worked for the US government, but I didn't believe him."

"He's with the FBI and was very interested in how you and I knew each other."

"We need to get out of here."

"And go where?"

"Not sure. I... I need to protect you."

"What you need to do is clear your name. Disappearing with me isn't a great strategy in that regard."

"I know, but I couldn't risk him hurting you."

"Look, stop." She took his hand. "I'm okay. I'm with you and we're both okay. But the threats will keep coming until you prove you're not a criminal."

"How am I supposed to do that while protecting you from these violent men?"

"We'll put our heads together and—"

"We? You're going back to the ranch where you'll be safe."

"Where will you go?"

"I'll disappear out here."

"Without a jacket, camping gear and supplies?"

"I'll figure it out."

"I'm sure you can but let me help."

He shook his head. "Where I go, trouble follows. I won't allow you to be an accessory to whatever I'll be charged with. The official story is I took you against your will."

She opened her mouth to protest.

"Please?"

"Okay, for now, until we figure out who we can trust. In the meantime, we need a safe place to hide out. I've got an idea about that."

They continued hiking, Rose leading the way to this mysterious place she said could serve as a temporary, safe refuge.

Every minute that passed, Noah became even more on edge than the last. He was a target and Rose was standing right next to him, which made her a target as well.

He thought about Detective Harper being shot, and how the bullet could have been meant for Noah.

"This is going to be interesting," Rose said.

"What?"

She pointed to a rope bridge in the distance that spanned across the river below. "The bridge used to be in a lot better shape when we were kids."

"Is there another way to get where we're going?"

"This bridge is a shortcut that will bring us down to the Brewer Ranch, where I'm house-sitting. Otherwise it's another four hours, and it's going to be dark in two. This is the best option."

Noah was amazed by her ability to charge into

a potentially hazardous situation without much hesitancy. She would have made a good soldier.

"I heard teenagers from Boulder Creek High had been out here," she said as they got closer to the bridge. "Their parents would be furious if they knew the kids were playing on that thing."

"I suspect your parents won't be too happy, either."

"I won't tell if you don't." She winked.

"How do you do that?"

"What, wink?"

"After everything you've been through, you still have a sense of humor."

"Wouldn't have survived without it. Well, that and my faith."

"Yeah, sometime you'll have to explain that to me."

"Faith?"

He nodded.

"You know how it works."

"No, I don't. I wasn't raised in a religious home, and the things I saw in combat, the things I did..." His voice trailed off and he shook his head.

"Noah, God forgives. Believe that. As for the faith part, you're committed to your faith."

"How's that?"

"You believe so strongly in your friend that you came out here to find him and help him, even when it put your life at risk. That's faith, Noah."

"I never thought about it that way."

"It's the same thing, but you direct your faith toward a higher power, a loving and merciful God who loves you."

They approached the bridge and she hesitated. "I'm going to message the SAR team leader that I'm okay."

"But—"

"Otherwise, they'll waste time and manpower trying to find me. I'll tell him I headed back down."

Noah glanced both ways, scanning the area on their side of the river, and on the other side. It hit him what easy targets they would be as they crossed the wooden-planked bridge, out in the open for all to see.

"What is it?" she said. "Is this triggering memories?"

"No, but we're going to be very exposed."

"Then let's do it quickly. Ready?"

"I'll go first to check for weak or broken boards," he said.

"Okay. Keep both hands on the railing in case your foot falls through."

He glanced below at the robust river. He wasn't frightened for himself, but the thought of Rose falling—

"Hey, get out of your head. Let's go," she said, and started to go around him.

He put out his hand, and stepped onto the bridge. The sound of rushing water grounded him, as he kept his eyes on the boards ahead, looking for damaged ones to avoid.

"Noah!" Rose called out.

He glanced over his shoulder.

She was fine, walking sideways so she could keep both hands on the handrail. She nodded, encouraging him to do the same.

He saw the wisdom in that tactic and followed her direction. He would be on the lookout for any loose boards, take a few steps and glance behind him, making sure Rose mimicked his exact moves. Heart racing, he wished he could hold on to her to make sure she was safe but knew that would come with its own set of problems, the first of which being the distraction. He needed to stay focused on his objective: get to the other side safely with Rose.

About two-thirds of the way across, he glanced back at Rose to see if she was still doing okay. She nodded that she was.

He held her gaze for a moment longer than necessary; thought she might have even smiled.

She took a step.

Gasped with panic.

"Noah!"

EIGHT

Rose's heart leaped into her throat.

A man was heading toward them from the other side of the bridge.

"Behind you!" she shouted.

Noah turned as the man charged, tackling Noah on the weakened bridge. They both struggled for dominance. The bridge swayed from side to side, Rose gripping the rail with both hands for support.

She quickly calculated how she could help Noah. Bear spray. She had bear spray in her pack. She took off her pack and pulled out the spray. Got the pack back on her shoulder, and edged closer to the men, one arm firmly around the railing.

The attacker, a heavyset man in a dark jacket and black ski cap, had pinned Noah on his stomach with a knee against his lower back.

She knew what it felt like to be pinned, helpless.

"Get off!" she shouted.

Instead, the guy wrapped his arm around Noah's neck and squeezed. Noah gasped, digging his fingers into the guy's arm.

"I mean it!" she said, aiming the bear spray with one hand, while clinging to the railing with the other.

The guy looked up, a wicked glint in his eye. He gave Noah's neck another squeeze, and released him. Noah's body went limp.

He couldn't have killed him in that short period of time.

If he had, he certainly would have no qualms about killing Rose.

"Rose, right?" the guy said, taking a step toward her.

"Don't come any closer!" She held out the spray in front of her.

"Didn't anyone ever tell you not to help criminals?"

He lunged as she fired the spray, but he batted it out of her hand before she could nail him. He grabbed her wrist and leaned close, too close.

Rage bubbled up inside.

He said something to her, she wasn't sure what, and it didn't matter.

This, she had trained for.

Hit the most vulnerable spots first.

She kneed him in the groin. He stumbled back.

Crack.

A weak board gave way. The guy fell through as Noah scrambled to get to him. Rose edged toward the missing board beside Noah and saw their attacker facedown on a rock in the river below.

He'd threatened her and nearly killed Noah, but Noah's instinct was still to try and save him from falling to his death.

"C'mon, before more guys show up," she said, glancing at the other end of the bridge. There wouldn't be only one of these creeps out here, right? It seemed like they came in pairs at least.

Noah didn't respond and continued to stare at the motionless body.

"Noah?" she encouraged.

They needed to move and fast.

"C'mon, soldier, the enemy's close."

He finally looked at her with piercing blue eyes. "The enemy?"

"I doubt that guy was alone. Can you walk?"

He nodded that he could. She helped him stand and they continued to cross the bridge to the other side. Rose packed away that she saw a man fall to his death. Her priority had to be getting herself and Noah out of harm's way. Once safe, she'd call the police and let them know what had happened.

Only, how could she report the death without revealing Noah's location?

She'd worry about that later. Right now, they had to get to the Brewer Ranch before dark so they could regroup, figure out next steps.

Noah had his arm around her shoulder leaning on her for support. Her adrenaline must be pumping like crazy because she hardly felt the weight. They hiked in silence, both probably thinking the same thing: that the guy from the Woodland Bridge was undoubtedly not alone.

"Victor!" a man called out.

Rose led Noah into a cluster of trees off the trail. They stood very still, out of sight. She focused on slow, deep breathing. When Noah closed his eyes, she feared the attack had triggered traumatic memories. His breathing was slow and steady, so that was a good sign.

"Victor! Where are you!" The man was closer, probably just on the other side of the trees.

"Victor!" another man called out.

There were two of them.

She heard the sound of men panting as they hurried toward the bridge.

As a few minutes passed, she tried to assuage her panic by counting her blessings: Noah was okay, she was okay. They weren't killed by the man named Victor, and once they escaped his partners, she and Noah would find refuge at the Brewer Ranch, where they could recover together.

Together? Sure, but not *really* together she reminded herself.

In the meantime, how long would they have to wait for the danger to pass?

"Down there!"

Rose peered around the trees and spotted one of the guys stepping onto the bridge. She fisted her hand, wanting to call out to be careful, but not wanting to expose their position to men who would potentially shoot them on sight.

She watched as one of the men tried crossing the bridge.

"It's too dangerous!" the other called.

He backed up and the men hovered above the river, trying to figure out the best way to get to Victor. One of the men tied rope around a tree and disappeared from view. They were going to rappel down to the river.

The other guy gripped the rope and followed his partner. Once they were out of sight, she turned to Noah.

"You okay?"

He nodded.

They returned to the trail and went north, toward the Brewer Ranch.

"It's a little tricky when we come back down in about half a mile," she said.

"When we get to the ranch, I'll turn myself in."

"Noah—"

"I can't keep putting you in danger. The guy on the bridge could have—"

"He didn't. I'm fine. You're fine."

"Because you saved me," he said, with an edge to his voice.

"You're welcome?" she said.

"I owe you my life. All that matters now is keeping you safe."

"In case you haven't noticed, I'm pretty good at keeping myself safe."

"I have noticed. And I'm ashamed."

"What? Why?"

"I'm not sure how to put an end to this to get your normal, safe life back."

"After what we've been through, my normal life seems pretty boring," she teased.

He snapped his attention to her.

"What?" she said.

"Your sense of humor, it throws me off sometimes."

"Sorry, it keeps me grounded. What's our next move?"

"I'm conflicted. I need to find Thomas, but I'm more worried about you."

"I wish everyone would stop worrying about me." She sidestepped a tree root on the trail.

"Who's everyone?"

"My family treated me like the fragile baby who always needed their help."

"They love you."

"*Love*, yeah, a strange word for an emotion that's very complicated."

"Ex-boyfriend?"

"You mean Detective Harper? He was basically dating me to make up for my sister's death." She snapped her attention to him. "Sorry, TMI."

"I doubt that was his only motive. You're a smart, sweet and beautiful woman."

"Wow, thanks. Anyway, I couldn't be sure if T.J. was interested in me for me, or if he dated me to make up for Cassie's death since he was supposed to be with her the night of her accident. Rather than drag it out, I broke it off so we could both get on with our lives."

"And have you? Moved on?"

"From T.J.? Yes. Only I feel like I've been holding back with other stuff, the direction in life, kinda coasting." She glanced at him. "Sorry, this feels like more airplane therapy."

"If it helps to talk about it…"

"To a stranger, right."

"We're not exactly strangers, Rose."

"No, I guess not."

"So…?" he prompted.

"When you keep getting the message that you can't do anything on your own, or make good decisions, which that high school incident proved, you start to believe it. Even when I moved away as an adult, I avoided relying on others because I wanted to prove I could do everything on my own. Not need help from anyone, especially a guy."

They hiked in silence for a few minutes, and she noticed Noah scan the forest behind them to see if they were being followed.

"I should stop talking so you can focus on whatever danger awaits us out there," she said.

"I can do two things at once. Go ahead, keep

talking, if you want to. This plane passenger is enjoying the discussion."

"Hey, you did it. You used your sense of humor."

Then he winked at her. She felt herself blush.

"Did you have a boyfriend in the city, friends?" he said.

"Yeah. Boyfriend turned out to be a jerk. Inconsistent moods, critical at times. My roommate caught him on a dating site and clued me into his extracurricular activities with other women. Apparently, he liked meeting new ladies on the side. As for friends, I kept being drawn to people who wanted to take care of me, recreating my family, I guess. Once I figured that out, I started looking for friends who respected boundaries and wanted to support but not manage me. I looked for people like me, I guess."

"Smart and sweet."

"Stop complimenting me."

"Why?"

"It makes me uncomfortable."

"You act like you don't deserve it."

"If I seem sweet, it's probably because I'm a people pleaser, and if I was smart I would have done something more important with my life, been more like my sister."

"What did she do?"

"Managed accounts at a marketing firm."

"What makes that more important than training dogs to be loving and obedient pets, taking care of people's homes when they're away and helping out with your family?"

"Or your career as a... What's your title again?"

"Tech Security Specialist."

"See, that sounds impressive."

"It's a job, and some days it requires me to sit and stare at a computer screen for hours. The grass isn't always greener, Rose."

"What about doctors? They do something amazingly worthwhile. They save lives."

"That's an awfully high bar."

"I'm just saying."

"They also graduate with massive debt, and have to deal with accountability metrics like fitting appointments into twenty-minute blocks of time."

"My ex-roommate was a paralegal," she tried again.

"Which is great if you love the law, and I'm sure there's plenty of mundane office work involved with that, too. Do you love the law, Rose?"

"Not particularly. What inspired you to go into tech?"

"I didn't have to be social." He shot her a smile. "That, and preventing cyberattacks by shutting down the bad guys."

"And Thomas?"

"Thomas was always about justice. Which is

why the accusations about him selling software to the enemy is so wrong."

"Maybe someone set him up?"

"Maybe."

"Or…?"

"Maybe he got cocky and decided to take on the enemy without support. That wouldn't surprise me."

"Why would he do that? Wouldn't he at least ask for your help?"

"No, not if he feared things might go bad. He wouldn't want me to look culpable if it all blew up in his face."

"So, he was protecting you."

"Perhaps."

"Yet you threw yourself into the line of fire anyway."

"That's what you do for people you care about. I don't have an easy time making friends, but Thomas and I seemed to bond right away, and he saved my life more than once."

"In combat?"

"And back home. I was pretty lost when I returned stateside. He pulled me up and out of my funk and got me into school, then found me an internship at Stratosphere. When I graduated, they offered me a job because they were familiar with my skills and work ethic." He hesitated. "I'm not sure where I'd be if it hadn't been for Thomas."

"You should give yourself more credit. Thomas

didn't go to school and get the degree. You did. And they wouldn't have given you a job if you weren't qualified. I'm not downplaying the importance of his encouragement, but you were a big part of that equation, right?"

"I suppose."

"He offered you a way out and you took it. You didn't have to. But still, I can see why you're so devoted to him."

"I have to help him. He's a good man."

"So are you, Noah."

More than an hour later, Rose said they were close to the ranch she was taking care of for vacationing owners. During the course of their hike, they talked on and off, drifting into companionable silence, then starting up a new subject. It almost seemed like they were good friends on a recreational adventure, which felt strange, but unusually grounding.

A feeling that seemed to normally elude Noah. Not good. He was developing a connection to this woman, maybe even a dependence that could only bring disaster to both their lives. He knew what he was: a damaged man who'd crossed the line into darkness too many times to ever justify redemption. No, not even Rose's God could forgive Noah. He knew this in his heart.

Yet she'd called him a good man.

Good? Noah would never classify himself as

good. Not after everything he'd done. But he didn't argue with Rose to avoid conflict between them.

Another red flag—he wanted her to be happy, to make her smile, maybe even laugh.

What was happening to him?

"Down there, see?" She pointed.

In the distance was a two-story house with a wraparound porch, a barn on the property and a pen for horses.

"They have livestock?"

"Yes. They're paying a local wrangler to care for the horses, pick stalls and feed them. Take them out in the pen for exercise."

"But no one's in the house?"

"No, that's my job. Make sure it looks lived in."

"Are you staying there?"

"Some nights there, some nights at my apartment, some nights at Mom and Dad's house. It's good for Oscar to learn how to be comfortable in different environments."

"He seems like he can be comfortable anywhere."

"Wasn't always that way. He can be a bit… neurotic, I guess."

They approached the back end of the trail that led to the property and she put up her hand. "I'll check it out first, to be sure."

"*I'm* protecting *you*, remember?"

She nodded. "Let's go."

The setting sun cast a burnt orange glow across the sky. She hurried toward the house as if she were on a mission and wasn't about to be deterred. He hoped they were alone, that the wrangler wasn't on the premises.

They made it to the back porch. "I have keys for the front. Wait here," she said.

She went to the front of the house and he waited for what seemed like forever. As he scanned the surrounding forest, he found himself grateful for his safety, and Rose's.

As the minutes passed, he grew worried and edged his way around the porch to the front.

"Thanks for letting me know, Adam," she said. "I'll call Mr. Brewer and give him the scoop when I check in with him tonight."

"No problem. I'll be out here tomorrow morning to exercise the horses. If Spirit is still punk, I'll call the vet."

"Sounds good. Oh, and could you do me a favor?"

"Sure."

"Don't tell anyone you saw me here tonight."

"Everything okay?"

"Yes, thanks for asking."

"But no car, no dog?"

"I was on a nature walk and decided to come the back way. My brother is picking me up later."

"Sounds good."

"Thanks so much."

Noah plastered himself up against the wall to stay out of sight. His presence would be hard to explain and could start rumors about Rose bringing a strange man to the Brewer Ranch. Noah heard a car start up so he went around back and waited.

Rose opened the back door. "C'mon in but wait in the kitchen for a few minutes."

"Until Adam's gone?"

"How did you—"

"I overheard part of your conversation. You were taking a long time and I was worried something might have happened to you."

"Adam's a dad-type and likes to chat. He's the wrangler Mr. Brewer paid to exercise the horses. One of them is acting strange so Adam might call the vet tomorrow. Anyway, I'll close the drapes. Be right back."

As Rose went into the front room, Noah turned on the kitchen sink to douse his face with water. It wasn't as much to clean the sweat of the day off his skin as to clear his muddled head and figure out his most important goals. Things were changing; his goals seemed to be changing.

Protecting Rose was his number one concern, then finding Thomas.

Should he work with authorities? Perhaps he'd be forced to in order to keep Rose safe.

There were too many enemies out there, and he

didn't want to continue putting Rose at risk. This lovely, kind, generous woman deserved to be safe.

Was he betraying his friend by making Rose's safety his priority? No, Thomas would do the same thing if he was in Noah's position. Thomas was about battling the enemy while keeping innocents out of harm's way.

When possible. Which was not always the case.

In truth, Noah's new goal was to put an end to the manhunt, which would both help Thomas by allowing him to come out of hiding and help Rose by keeping her safe from men who were hunting Noah and Thomas.

Rose just happened to get in the way. Her good, Christian nature put her there.

The sound of Rose's voice drifted to him from the living room.

"We're okay now, but it was tricky for a while there... Yeah, the old Woodland Bridge."

She must be talking to her family back at Boulder Creek Ranch. Noah entered the living room and she looked up. She was twirling strands of dark hair around her forefinger, a habit he'd noticed before.

"I texted Simon that I'm okay so they wouldn't waste time looking for me... I need you to keep this to yourself until we figure out who we can trust... I understand, Mom. Is Beau around? I need to talk to him, too."

Rose glanced at Noah and rolled her eyes.

"Hey, Beau. Noah said Agent Hart on the SAR team was one of the guys who took him from the hospital so Noah pulled me away from the group because he thought I was in danger... Yeah... We're fine but not sure who to trust... T.J.? Still not sure... I get that but... Beau, calm down. I could use your help, not your censure. Okay, text me later."

She ended the call. "Beau's going to keep up with SAR progress, and covertly reach out to T.J."

"You didn't tell your parents about the man who attacked us and fell through the bridge?"

"No, I didn't want to freak them out. It would get them whipped up and cause Dad to saddle up Boomer and ride over to rescue me."

"You told them where you're staying?"

"Yes, eventually they'd remember I'm taking care of things here and would figure it out. With Beau, it's better to include him from the beginning rather than have him go hunting for answers and feel out of the loop. He really loses it when he thinks people have been keeping things from him. It probably stems from the whole Harriet business."

"Harriet. He mentioned her the other night."

"They grew rather close when she stayed with us. She needed refuge from a violent home life and Mom secretly brought her to the ranch. She stayed with us for a couple of months, under the radar. Anyway, Harriet left the ranch without giving Beau a proper goodbye. He returned from a trail ride and she was gone."

"Ouch."

"Yeah, then he found out Mom and Dad knew she was leaving, and didn't tell him. It's not like they were keeping anything from him. They assumed Harriet told Beau about her plans to move to Colorado, but she didn't. I think she feared he'd try and talk her out of leaving, or he'd go after her."

"Would that have been a bad thing?"

"Well, and I'm only surmising here, she'd been traumatized by domineering, abusive men. Beau is in no way abusive, but he can be rather bossy. I'm guessing Harriet needed to get away and heal on her own, without a man guiding her. And Beau, well, he was in love with her, and wanted to protect her, which can come off as controlling. I'm living proof of that."

"You mean…?"

"My family. They wanted to protect me, but it felt oppressive and controlling. So, I could see where Harriet was coming from. It took a long time for Beau to recover from what he considered a betrayal."

"How long ago did this happen?" Noah asked.

"Fifteen years ago? Something like that."

"And he's never dated since?"

"Oh, he's dated, sure. He even got serious once, but couldn't bring himself to propose. I hate to say it, but Harriet might have been his one and only, if you believe in that sort of thing."

"Do you believe in that sort of thing?"

"I'm not sure. I know love can be complicated, that's for sure."

"Thank you for sharing that story. It helps me understand your brother better."

"Enough about our family drama. What's next on our list of ways to avoid danger?"

Noah sat at the dining table. "I wish I had a computer, or some way to track Thomas. Then I could hand you off to your parents and go find him."

"Hand me off, huh?" She sat across from him.

"That didn't come out right, sorry."

"Did you ever consider that Thomas may not want to be found?"

"By the Feds and Stratosphere Center, sure, but he wouldn't mind me coming to help."

"Maybe he doesn't want help."

"Why do you say that?"

"Because he's trying to protect you? If he wanted you involved in whatever was going on, he would have included you long before now, don't you think?"

"I guess."

"But...?"

"I saw him, Rose. At least I think I saw him."

"When?"

"When you found me at the riverbank. The

other guy was about to shoot me, and Thomas pulled him off."

She frowned.

"Maybe I was hallucinating. That's what I thought at first. But what if I wasn't?"

"What did he say?"

"He asked if I was hurt. Then he told me to go home."

"If it was Thomas and he wants you to leave, it sounds like *he* doesn't want to put *you* in danger."

"I get that, especially because Thomas tends to be stubbornly independent, always the giver, not the taker. Doesn't want to depend on anyone else."

"That's what makes you good friends. You understand each other."

"The reason I don't depend on anyone is because I never had that kind of support in my life, until Thomas." He hesitated, fiddled with the edge of a newspaper on the dining room table, then looked up. "And you."

As she struggled to come up with a response, a car door slammed outside.

"It's probably Beau." She stood, welcoming the break in their conversation. This was getting intense, Noah revealing his vulnerability and his appreciation, and Rose struggling to keep her boundary firm: he was a stranger who needed help, not a potential love interest. There were too many barriers for that to ever happen between them. Besides the obvious one of geography, she also had to consider the fact he didn't respect his friend's request to stay away. Noah acted as if he knew better than Thomas, and Rose could see this particular personality trait causing major conflict between her and Noah. If Rose were to become romantically involved again, it would be with someone who would respect her space, her decisions, and not try to manage her like family and friends had in the past. What was it about Rose that made people think she needed to rely on them?

She approached the window and peered outside. A truck was parked out front. Not Beau's truck.

The back doors of the truck opened, and two men got out.

The motion light clicked on.

A stranger stepped onto the front porch and withdrew a gun.

NINE

Noah waited in the kitchen, figuring Rose would need time to talk her brother down from his anger ledge. Beau's sister was in danger again, and her brother would no doubt blame Noah. A justified reaction.

Instead of hearing voices in a heated discussion from the other room, Rose darted into the kitchen.

"What's going—"

She put her forefinger to his lips to silence him, and led him into the kitchen pantry. She used her phone to illuminate the confined space bordered by canned goods and jarred preserves.

"Three men," she whispered. "The one at the door had a gun."

And she'd pulled them into a foxhole with no escape. At least if they'd fled through the back door—

He caught himself. She made the best decision she could, given the circumstances. The threat was close, probably too close to run and not be noticed. He still had his firearm, taken off the gunman at the bridge, but he'd left it on the kitchen table.

Three guys against Noah. Odds were not good.

But he had to defend himself, and more importantly save Rose.

"I need the gun," he whispered and reached out to open the door.

She grabbed his wrist and looked up at him. Shook her head, fear coloring her eyes.

"I'm a soldier, remember? I know how to do this."

"Wait, they'll go away."

"Hello!" someone called from the living room.

"They're inside?" she said.

He pulled her into a hug for comfort. He was outnumbered, so chances were this was going to go bad rather quickly. He'd do his best to neutralize the guys, or at least lead them away from Rose.

"Stay…here." He released her and cracked open the pantry door. Waited.

"You sure this is the right place?" a man said, his voice familiar. He was still in the front of the house, so Noah took the opportunity to exit the pantry.

He darted into the kitchen and grabbed the gun. The back door handle rattled. Someone was trying to get in.

Enemies were coming from both sides.

He clutched the gun.

Fought the images of war, the trauma that surfaced every time his heart rate sped up. His pulse pounded in his ears. The first sign he was about to be sucked into the vortex of terror.

No, I will not let it consume me. Not with Rose's life at risk.

He focused on his box breathing. Four, four, four, four.

If the guy got inside back here…

Too close, too close to Rose.

The back door opened.

Noah aimed the gun and shouted, "Drop the gun!"

Instead of the guys from the motel, or even the gray-haired agent standing there…

Noah was looking at army buddy Michael James, who slowly raised his hands.

"Michael?" Noah said.

No, this wasn't possible. Noah must be having a doozy of a flashback.

"Hey, buddy, long time, huh? Would you… uh…mind pointing that somewhere else?" He nodded at the gun.

When Noah didn't lower his weapon, the man's friendly expression melted into a sad frown.

"It can't be Michael James," Noah said, more to himself to keep things clear. "Michael is in Alaska."

"Too dark, too depressing, even for me," he said. "I moved back to Nashville last year."

"Hey, Noah," a man said from the living room doorway.

Noah spun around and aimed at…

Willy Rankin, another member of their unit that fought together in Afghanistan. Willy put up his hands. "I've got Chris Walsh here, too."

"Hey, Noah," a voice said from the living room.

"I don't understand," Noah said.

"Thomas texted us. Said you were in trouble so… Here we are."

Common sense warred with trauma, distrust of these men, distrust of Noah's own mind. Was it playing tricks on him?

"Friends till the end and beyond," Michael said.

"Friends till the end and beyond," Noah softly repeated.

A motto shared by army buddies who'd barely made it out alive.

"So, how was it?" Willy asked Noah.

Noah studied him.

"Your first meal stateside? Waffle House All-Star Special, hash browns, smothered and covered, right? As good as you remembered?" Willy said.

A memory flashed across Noah's mind: the five of them discussing their first meals when they returned home.

"Italian beef, sweet and dipped, with cheddar, large fries," Noah repeated Willy's choice.

"You got it, man. My favorite sandwich at Portillo's," Willy confirmed.

No one could know these intimate details but the men of his unit. Noah slowly lowered the gun.

"I... I'm sorry," he said, placing the gun on the kitchen table.

"Don't be." Willy approached Noah and gave him a hug.

"We're good!" Michael called out to Chris, who joined them.

Noah shared hugs with his other two friends and apologized again.

"Forget it," Willy said. "Sounds like you're in the heat of battle, so it's good to be extra cautious."

"What's going on?" Michael said. "Thomas's text was too cryptic for me to figure out."

"I came out here to find him, to help Thomas, but now my priority is protecting a friend." Noah went to the pantry and opened the door. Rose clenched a can of beans in her hand, as if preparing to brain him with it. "It's okay, Rose." He removed the can from her fingers and placed it on the shelf, then led her into the kitchen.

"Rose, meet my army buddies. Guys, this is Rose Rogers. She saved my life, more than once."

Each one of them shook Rose's hand and introduced themselves.

"Wow, talk about backup." She motioned them to sit at the kitchen table. Noah remained standing, still in disbelief.

"What are you doing here?" she asked.

Willy glanced at Noah.

"Go ahead. She has a right to know," Noah said.

"We three got a text from Thomas, ma'am. He said Noah was in trouble and needed our help. When we met up at the Missoula airport, he sent another text giving us these coordinates."

"How could he possibly know where we are?" Rose said.

"He must be tracking you somehow," Willy said.

"Thomas is brilliant like that," Chris offered.

"Yeah, a brilliant idiot," Michael chimed in.

"Hey," Willy admonished.

"What? He can be, and we all know it. If he wasn't so cocky, he probably wouldn't have gotten Noah in trouble."

"It was my choice to follow him out here," Noah said.

"I stand corrected," Michael said. "You're both idiots."

"Don't mind him, ma'am," Willy said to Rose. "He's tired and hungry."

"I wish I could cook something for all of us, but this isn't my house. I'm taking care of things while the owners are away."

"No worries. We stopped by a grocery on our way here. Would you mind if we brought in dinner supplies?"

"Sure."

Willy motioned to Michael and Chris, and they went to retrieve groceries.

"Again, sorry about Michael's attitude," Willy said. "He and Thomas were always going at it."

"I'm actually surprised Michael's with you," Noah said.

"He's…between jobs."

Which was code for Michael having lost another job, probably due to battle trauma or his smart mouth.

"What's the endgame here?" Noah said. "Take me back home?"

"Discuss, assess and strategize. First we need to figure out how severe the threat is and if it's safe to travel."

"I was supposed to be taken into custody by the Feds," Noah said.

"We can't trust them," Rose offered. "That's about where we were when you showed up, trying to figure out who to call for help and who we can trust."

Willy put out his hands, as if saying, *Here we are.*

"What do we know?" Willy said, as Michael and Chris reentered the kitchen carrying two bags of groceries.

"Feds claim Thomas was brokering a deal to sell specialized software that would give foreign agents access to US servers."

"That's—"

"Hey, lady present." Chris nudged Michael before he could finish his thought.

"Sorry, ma'am," Michael apologized. "But that's ridiculous. Thomas loves his country and would do everything in his power to protect it, not expose it to our enemies."

"That's what I told them when they questioned me back in Virginia," Noah said. "I went to Thomas's apartment. It was ransacked and I was assaulted, but the guys got away. The Feds brought me in for questioning. After that I sensed they were keeping me under surveillance. Worried about Thomas, I decided to come out here and find him to make sure he was okay."

"How'd that go?" Willy said.

"I was either followed from Virginia, or they were already here looking for him, found out I was coming to town and decided to use me to track him."

"Who are 'they'?" Chris asked.

"The first two guys were from Stratosphere, where we work," Noah said.

"They found Noah in the mountains and again at his motel," Rose offered. "Then two other men took him from the hospital."

"Claimed to be federal agents," Noah said. "Technically I went with them to divert them from hurting innocent people. They nearly killed an orderly right in front of me."

"Federal agents don't kill civilians," Willy said.

"They're not supposed to anyway," Michael piped up.

"These guys were determined to find Thomas."

"Two teams, one from work and one from the Feds?" Willy said.

"Then there was the guy who attacked us on the bridge and his partners," Rose said.

"And whoever shot the detective when he was transporting me to meet with the Feds," Noah added. "We're not sure who that was."

"Any guesses?" Willy asked.

"Probably whichever foreign country is trying to obtain Thomas's software. If they get me, they're that much closer to Thomas. I suspect when I came to Montana I gave all the players the impression I was meeting up with him."

"Do you know where he is?" Willy said.

"A general idea," Noah said.

"Very general," Rose added.

Michael snickered.

"I know one thing for sure," Noah said. "He's in danger and he needs our help."

Rose called Mr. Brewer to ask his permission for Noah to stay on the property. When she shared the story about Noah, a traumatized veteran being stalked by violent men, Mr. Brewer invited Noah and his friends to use his house as their home base until they achieved victory. It turned out

Mr. Brewer was a Gulf War veteran and wanted to support his fellow soldiers.

"Wow, that's very generous," Rose said. "You don't even know them."

"They fought for our country. That's all I need to know."

"They'll be very grateful. How are things in Florida?"

"Good. Looks like we're buying a place down here. Going to sell the ranch and make retirement official."

"Congratulations."

"Well, I wish we could have kept the ranch going, but these days it's too much for an old guy like me. If only I could sell the place to someone who loves Montana as much as I do, not to a conglomerate that'll turn my beautiful land into a posh resort or strip mall."

"Yeah, I get it."

"A real estate developer has already reached out, but it doesn't feel right. Anyway, thanks again for taking care of the place."

"My pleasure."

"I'll text Adam that some friends are bunking at the ranch so he's on board," Mr. Brewer said. "Tell those vets they are welcome to stay as long as necessary."

"Aren't you coming back next Tuesday?"

"We've extended our stay an extra week. Does that work with your schedule?"

"Sure, no problem."

"Thanks."

"No, thank you for being so generous with your home. Bye."

Rose wandered back into the kitchen and spotted Chris giving Michael a playful shove. "Mr. Brewer said you can stay here if you'd like."

"Great, we'll pitch our tents out back," Willy said.

"I think he meant inside," Rose said.

"Thanks, but we like the fresh air," Willy said.

Sudden pounding on the front door startled her.

She headed out of the kitchen and Noah touched her shoulder. "I'm right behind you."

"It's probably my dad with Oscar."

She went to the door, peered through the lace curtains and spotted Beau's back. Oh boy. She said a quick prayer for patience and opened the door. Oscar dashed inside and began sniffing the room.

Before she could get a word out, Beau stormed past her, not seeing Noah standing beside the door.

"You still think this was a good idea?" Beau challenged, marching toward the kitchen. Oscar raced up to Noah, wagging his tail.

"Being kidnapped from a search mission," Beau muttered.

"I wasn't kidnapped. I was led away for my own safety."

"Is that the story he's telling? Greene, where are you?" Beau approached the kitchen doorway and froze at the sight of Noah's friends. "Who are these guys?"

"We served together in Afghanistan," Noah said, coming up behind Beau and entering the kitchen. Oscar trotted behind him and greeted each of the veterans.

"And they're here why?" Beau said.

"Who's this guy?" Michael asked Noah.

"Bossy brother," Rose answered.

"I'm not bossy," Beau said, motioning her out of the kitchen. "I'm worried. I'm allowed, okay? I've already lost one sister. I can't lose you, too."

The house went silent.

Rose led him to the living room sofa and sat with him. "I'm sorry."

"So, you admit you're making bad choices."

"No, I'm sorry for your pain, Beau. I feel it too, the grief of losing Cassie. What's happening here is different."

"You've chosen to attach yourself to a violent man—"

"It's not Noah who's violent, it's the situation. I didn't go out on an SAR training mission the other day looking for trouble, but while out there I found a wounded man who needed help. I could not walk away from that, and you wouldn't have wanted me to."

"But this…" He motioned toward the kitchen. "You brought strangers into the Brewers' house?"

"Mr. Brewer approves of them being here and they're not strangers. They served with Noah and are here to help."

"You're coming home with me. Now."

Out of the corner of her eye, she saw Noah hovering in the kitchen doorway.

"Beau, I love you, but I'm not ten anymore."

"Okay, so you won't let me help you."

"I don't need this kind of help. I need you to believe in me."

He stood to leave.

Rose also stood. "Now, if you want to help us figure out who we can trust, and track down Thomas, well, that kind of help we could certainly use."

He turned to her.

"Think of it this way," she said. "You'll be keeping an eye on your little sister. C'mon."

She went into the kitchen, hoping he'd follow her. Noah offered a supportive nod, but his friends avoided her gaze. It was like they were giving her space.

The front door opened and shut. Her heart sank.

"Pardon my brother," she said. "He's a little overprotective."

"He's justified," Noah said. "If I thought leaving you right now would keep you out of danger

I would, but I'm a realist. There's already a target on your back and just like they're using me to get to Thomas, they'll use you to get to me."

"Okay, so how do we fix this?" Chris said. "What's the mission?"

The front door opened and shut again. A few seconds later, Beau entered the kitchen with a laptop. "Figured you could use one of these to help do research or whatever. It's got a VPN so they can't trace the ISP." He put the computer on the kitchen table.

The guys shared appreciative nods.

"I will do whatever it takes to keep my sister safe," Beau said, making eye contact with each and every one of them, finally ending with Noah.

"That makes two of us," Noah said. "Keeping Rose safe is my number one priority."

Willy stood and went to pour another cup of coffee. "Count us in."

"Good, now let's plan the mission," Noah said.

The next morning Rose awoke to the sound of muted voices downstairs. She'd slept in the guest room on the second floor, while Noah and his friends took turns sleeping in tents out back and standing guard in the house's front window.

She sat up in bed and glanced around. No Oscar. He must be having more fun with the guys than watching Rose sleep. She glanced at her phone, surprised and a little embarrassed that she'd slept until eight.

They'd been up late, Rose saying good-night around midnight, as the guys still hovered around the kitchen table brainstorming strategies for finding their friend with minimal danger, while keeping Noah and Rose out of harm's way.

Thankfully Beau had brought a bag Mom had packed with Rose's "extras," as Mom called them, clothes Mom kept handy in case Rose decided to spend the night at the ranch. Rose sensed that Mom was keeping a dream alive that her youngest daughter would move back in and become a permanent part of the Rogers clan.

Rose wasn't ready for that, and wasn't sure if she'd ever be. It felt like she was going backward if she sank into the fold of a family who tended to smother her. Although she knew it was motivated by love, until she could clearly articulate boundaries with Mom, Dad and Beau, she needed to keep her distance.

Last night she felt she'd done a pretty good job of speaking her truth to Beau, explaining in a compassionate tone that what she needed most was his support.

I need you to believe in me.

She'd never spoken the words before, nor had she admitted to herself how important it was for her family to respect her wishes. It was critical that they believed in her, even if on some days she struggled with her own confidence.

She showered and got dressed in a comfortable pair of jeans, long-sleeve cotton shirt and flannel shirt. Friday was her lightest day of the week, with only one private dog client, and one other property to check on. She'd have to cancel the private client but what about the Larsons' place? Maybe she could give Beau the code and he could swing by the house for her.

She felt guilty asking for the favor, but suspected Noah and his friends wouldn't want her out and about with the unclear threat hovering close by. Still, she felt a pang of frustration and disappointment in herself. Regardless of how her family perceived Rose, she prided herself on being a responsible business owner who followed through with her commitments. It was bad enough she had to cancel yesterday's appointments due to her current situation.

She brushed her hair, twisted it into a knot at the base of her neck and headed downstairs. The fleeting thought that she wished Mom had packed mascara and blush made Rose hesitate at the top of the stairs. She rarely wore makeup, so why was she thinking about it now?

Noah.

"You are losing it, girl." Because she wasn't

interested in attracting Noah. Their relationship wasn't like that. It was, in a word, different.

Indefinable. Complicated. Safe?

As she descended the stairs, she spotted Michael, the edgy veteran of the group, gazing out the window.

"Good morning," she said.

He didn't answer. He kept staring, fixated on something outside. Worry unfurled in her gut. Had their enemies discovered their location?

"What is it? What's wrong?"

"Huh?" Michael looked at her.

"Are we in danger?"

He seemed confused for a second.

"I said good morning, but you're so focused on something outside you didn't respond."

Michael glanced out the window, then back at Rose. "Oh, sorry, everything's fine."

She stepped up beside him to see for herself. Adam was out in the pen exercising one of the horses.

"I used to ride when I was a kid. Then we moved to the city," he said. "I loved horses."

"Go out there and ask Adam to saddle a horse for you."

"Nah, that's okay, I shouldn't get distracted. Chris made breakfast. He's a pretty good cook." He looked back outside.

She felt like she was intruding somehow, so

she went to the kitchen, where she was greeted by Chris and her brother.

"Where's Noah?" she said.

Beau raised his eyebrow.

"Stop," she said.

"I didn't say anything."

"Your eyebrow did." She poured herself a cup of coffee.

"I didn't know eyebrows could talk."

"Noah's outside with Willy," Chris said. "Organizing supplies for the hike."

"What hike?"

"Well, they're not going to find this Thomas guy by sitting around eating bacon and eggs," Beau said.

"Someone got up on the wrong side of the saddle," she countered. "Wait, you went home last night, right?"

He shook his head. "Sofa's comfortable enough."

"What about chores at the ranch?"

"Dad's got it covered."

"Beau, I didn't mean for you to—"

"I wanted to make sure you slept through the night without any more excitement. The guys have convinced me they're highly trained and can keep you safe."

"I thought you said they're heading into the mountains to find Thomas?"

"Me and Willy are," Chris said. "Noah and

Michael will stay back and keep watch over you. Willy identified Thomas's last known coordinates and we'll start there."

"And if you find him?"

"We'll convince him to come out of hiding and put an end to all this."

Beau stood. "I'll report back to Mom and Dad that you're fine. I'm heading to the ranch."

"Remember, we need to keep our location a secret," Chris said.

Beau shot him a look.

Chris put up his hands in surrender. "Didn't mean to offend."

"T.J. will probably want to follow up when he's released from the hospital," Beau said.

"Once we figure out who we can trust, Noah will reach out to the proper authorities. It's best if you act like you have no idea where your sister and Noah are," Chris reiterated.

"Heard you the first time."

"For your own safety as well as theirs."

Rose touched Beau's arm, not only to interrupt the power struggle between her brother and Noah's friend, but also to let him know how much she appreciated his presence. "Thank you, Beau."

"What, for being a bossy big brother?"

"For being an awesome, protective big brother." She smiled. "Truly."

With a slight grunt, he turned and left the kitchen.

"Bacon, eggs and hash browns?" Chris offered.

"That would be amazing, thanks. Where's Oscar?"

"Wherever Noah goes, Oscar goes."

On cue, Noah opened the kitchen door and Oscar rushed around him to greet Rose. "Hey, you." She stroked his head as he leaned against her legs, looking up at her with love in his eyes. "I hope you behaved."

"He did," Noah said.

They made eye contact and she sensed a calmness about him, almost as if his friends made him feel safe and grounded.

Her phone beeped with a text, and she glanced at it. The Kenmore Nursing Home was texting to confirm.

"Everything okay?" Noah asked.

Right, she'd forgotten about her first visit to the nursing home today, her foray into local volunteer work.

"One of the things I was supposed to do today."

"One of the things?" Noah asked.

"Well, I've got a private training with a golden doodle I can reschedule, and I need to check on the Larsons' house. Not a big deal. But my first nursing home visit with Oscar was scheduled for later this morning. I was looking forward to that. He always has a way of cheering people up, don't ya, buddy?"

"Yeah," Noah said. "He's good at that."

"I'd better reschedule. I figure I'm kind of stuck here for my own good."

Noah couldn't stand the defeated tone of her voice. His fault. His choices brought them to this place where she considered herself more like a prisoner than a friend.

Friend? Was that what they were?

No, it felt much deeper than that. She was a very good friend he could trust with his life.

"There could be worse places to hide out." Chris offered her a plate of food and she sat at the kitchen table.

Her expression seemed...resigned. Maybe even melancholy.

This woman hadn't been melancholy since Noah had met her. She'd been positive, asser-tive and brave. He refused to be the cause for her sadness.

"Does anyone else know your schedule for today?" Noah asked.

"No, well, except for my clients and the nurs-ing home."

"What are you thinking, Noah?" Chris said.

"I don't want Rose to forfeit her life because I got her into this mess."

"You didn't get me into anything. *I* found *you*, remember?"

"It's a good thing you did," Chris said.

"I can reschedule the dog training," Rose said.

"But you need to check on the house, and you want to visit the nursing home, right?"

Rose shrugged. "It's a trial run for my weekly visit."

"Then let's make that happen."

"But—"

"If we hide, they win. If we sacrifice things we love, they win. If you want, I'll turn myself in to authorities to take the bull's-eye off of you."

"Oh no you won't," Rose countered.

"He won't what?" Willy said, joining them.

"Turn himself in so my life can get back to normal."

Willy studied Noah. "You said that?"

Noah nodded.

"O-kay. Why does he need to turn himself in again?"

"Because he thinks it will take the bull's-eye off of Rose and then she can go about her life," Chris offered.

Willy snorted. "Doubtful."

"There has to be a way for Rose to fulfill her commitments," Noah said, looking at Willy. "They know Rose's car, but not your rental. Has it got tinted back windows?"

"It does," Willy said.

"Good, then Michael drives. No one knows him, and we can stay hidden in the back until we reach our destination. That way Rose can still live her life."

"Hey, Mike, you good with playing chauffeur and bodyguard for Noah and Rose?"

"Sure!" he answered from the living room.

"Good. Chris and I are leaving in twenty," Willy said. "Everyone, be safe."

Rose had been a little anxious about the decision to leave the Brewer Ranch to both visit the nursing home and swing by the Larson place. Yet Noah and Michael were confident they could stay under the radar, especially if Noah remained out of sight.

When she, Oscar and Michael entered the nursing home, she was so appreciative that Noah had pushed her to follow through with the visit today. Some of the residents, who were gathered in the community room, cracked big smiles upon seeing the coltriever prance his way across the vinyl floor. The expressions on their faces warmed Rose's heart as each and every one of them petted Oscar and chatted with him and each other. It was experiences like these that made her feel centered.

Somehow Noah had known she needed this moment, so much so that he'd taken this risk of exposing them in order to help her achieve inner peace.

It seemed as if he knew her better than her

family, and her few friends. Then again, she'd shared intimate details of her life with Noah during their "airplane therapy" conversations, details she hadn't shared with anyone else.

After an hour in the community room, where Oscar charmed residents with his soulful expression and wagging tail, she stopped by a few private rooms to say hello. One woman discussed her childhood Boston terrier, Rocco, while another asked if Oscar would come back next week.

The event went smoothly, and the executive director asked if Rose could visit their other facility in Missoula, offering to pay a stipend to cover Rose's gas and travel time. Rose said she'd check her schedule and get back to her.

As they headed for the SUV, Rose said, "Hear that, Oscar? You're a superstar."

"You've got a good one there," Michael said.

"Which is funny because Oscar was surrendered due to his mischievous behavior."

"I'm referring to Noah."

She glanced at Michael.

"He took a big risk bringing you here today," Michael said.

"I know. And I deeply appreciate it."

"I've never known him to put anything before the mission." He caught her eye. "Be good to him."

"I will."

She understood his meaning: Noah had made

a choice to put her needs first, something a man had rarely, if ever, done for Rose. It felt different, but a nice kind of different.

Rose mattered, she was a priority. It felt amazing.

They reached the truck and Michael opened the back door.

Noah was gone.

TEN

Protect her. You must protect her.

Noah used parked cars as cover and made his way through the lot toward the back of the nursing home where the two men he recognized as Stratosphere agents had gone.

Heart pounding, Noah calmed the surge of adrenaline that could trigger an untimely episode. He couldn't lose his focus or self-control to battle scars.

He had to protect Rose.

Rushing into the building, he pressed his back against the wall and listened for any indication of the men's exact whereabouts. They'd exited their car and gone around back. A sure sign they planned to kidnap Rose.

Or maybe they assumed Noah was with her, and they were really after him.

He couldn't take that chance. He had to get to her, save her.

Like she'd saved him so many times in the past few days.

As he edged toward the corner of the building, he reminded himself that Michael was with her, that he wouldn't let anything happen to Rose.

Somehow that wasn't enough. Noah couldn't sit idly by in the SUV, waiting for something to happen.

Waiting for the guys to flee the scene with Rose as their hostage.

How did they find her?

He'd puzzle his way to an answer when they were safe. Right now he had to focus on the current mission: finding Rose.

Keeping her safe.

Why did she have to be the one to discover and protect Noah from the Stratosphere agents? She didn't deserve to have her life upended because of Noah's loyalty to Thomas.

Please, just go home, go back to Virginia.

Thomas's directive. He *had* been at the riverbank.

And ordered Noah to let it go and leave town.

If only he could, but there was no turning back. He'd involved an innocent woman in this mess, and she deserved to get her life back. Noah would stay in Boulder Creek to see this through to the end, no matter what the resolution.

He took a quick breath and turned the corner. No one was there. He slowly approached the exit.

Reached for the door.

And was grabbed from behind. A firm arm snaked around his neck, as his attacker yanked Noah's right arm behind his back.

"Told you he'd show up," a man said.

"Let's get out of here," his partner answered.

Noah struggled against the firm hold.

The second guy got in his face. "Stop fighting or we'll take your lady friend, too."

"She's not involved," Noah croaked against the choke hold.

"Oh yes I am." Rose stepped around the corner of the building.

"Rose…" Noah gasped.

"Release him!" she ordered.

"Aren't you a spunky one?" The taller guy started toward her, while the other guy kept a firm hold on Noah.

Rose disappeared around the corner. Noah pleaded with Rose's God. *Protect her, don't let any harm come to her.*

"Where you going, Spunky?" The tall agent followed her around the corner.

With what little breath he had left, Noah tried elbowing his assailant, but the guy dodged the blow and yanked on Noah's arm even more. Noah stomped on his foot and the stranglehold loosened, but not enough.

"Knock it off," the guy said, applying pressure to Noah's throat.

With his free hand, Noah dug his fingers between the guy's arm and Noah's neck, trying to get air. Stars floated across his vision. The guy lowered him to his knees and applied more pressure. Noah's vision blurred.

Rose. He had to save Rose.

The guy suddenly released him. Noah collapsed to his hands and knees, gasping for air. Had to stay conscious. He shook his head, trying to clear his vision, his thoughts.

"It's okay, you're okay," Rose said, stroking his back.

He glanced sideways into the most beautiful pair of green eyes. She was there. She was okay.

He heard grunting behind him, and he guessed Michael had neutralized the man pursuing Rose and was doing the same to the guy who'd almost choked Noah into unconsciousness.

A moment later, the assailant collapsed beside Noah on the ground.

"We've gotta go. They won't be out for long." Michael helped Noah stand and the three of them hurried around the side of the building toward the SUV, passing the unconscious Stratosphere agent.

They reached the vehicle and Noah climbed into the back, greeted by an excited Oscar.

"Who were those guys?" Michael asked as they pulled away from the nursing home.

"Stratosphere agents."

"His own company sent these guys to find him? Why?"

"I'm guessing they want to bury this to save their reputation before word gets out their company allowed software to be leaked to foreign enemies," Noah said.

"And they keep coming after you…?"

"To flush out Thomas, or they think I'm somehow involved."

"Why did you leave the truck?" Rose asked.

"I saw them approach the building. I had to protect you."

"It looks like they used your need to protect Rose to lure you out into the open," Michael shot back.

"This has got to end," Rose said, petting Oscar. "Those men tried to kidnap you, three times now. Plus, there's the FBI agent, and the guys on the bridge. I'm calling T.J." She pulled out her phone.

"Rose." He placed his hand over hers. "We still don't know if we can trust him."

"I doubt they would have shot him if he was on their side. Noah, you have to start trusting people. At least, trust me. I know T.J."

He let his hand slide off hers and lowered his gaze.

"Look, I won't call if you don't want me to, but we need help from someone. Agent Hart is sketchy, so the Feds are out, but I know T.J. I've got an idea. I have to check on the Larsons' place. I'll contact T.J. and ask him to meet us there. We'll watch from the road. If he shows up alone, we'll know he can be trusted, okay?"

"Michael, what do you think?"

"Would be nice to have support from law enforcement instead of dodging them, too."

"Okay, but maybe we should drop Rose off at home first."

Rose sat back and crossed her arms over her chest. "That's not happening."

"Rose—"

"T.J. trusts me. Plus, you both promised my brother you'd stay close to me and keep me from harm. You can't do that if you're miles away."

"If T.J. brings trouble—"

"He won't. You know he's one of the good guys, or you wouldn't have risked your own life to save his at the lake."

Noah couldn't come up with a counterargument, so he nodded for her to make the call.

"Who knows if he's even out of the hospital," she muttered and called the detective. "Hey... Yes, I'm fine. How about your...? Oh good, I'm relieved to hear you're okay... I know, but... T.J.... Detective, would you *please* stop talking and listen to me?" She sighed. "I'm with Noah and a veteran friend of his. Two men tried to kidnap Noah from the Kenmore Nursing Home. They're probably still there if you want to send someone to... I was there for a visit with Oscar... It should have been safe but... They could have taken me, too." She shared a look with Noah.

Noah figured out her strategy: if Rose was in

danger, the detective was more likely to get involved than if the threat was just to Noah.

"We don't know who to trust. Agent Hart was one of the guys who took Noah from the hospital… I'm sure… Can you help us, without reporting it to the Feds for now anyway…? Good, okay, meet us at the Larson estate off of Cherry Hill Road… Just you… Until we know who to trust… See you then."

She nodded at Noah. "We're set to meet him in an hour."

"Let's not mention Willy and Chris's plan to find Thomas," Michael said from the front seat.

"Why not?" Rose said.

"Authorities won't like us meddling," Noah said. "How did those Stratosphere agents know where to find us, anyway?"

Michael passed his phone to Noah in the back seat. A social media post popped up: a resident of Kenmore Nursing Home smiling as she petted Oscar, Rose smiling in the background.

"An employee must have posted it," Michael said.

"Unbelievable." Noah passed the phone back.

"It's my fault. I never should have let you bring me here," Rose said.

"Not your fault," Noah said. "We couldn't have known an innocent post would expose our location."

"Still, it makes me wonder what other random,

completely out-of-our-control things might happen that will put us in danger. I'm so over it." She glanced out the window.

Noah placed his hand on her shoulder, and she turned to look at him.

"I'm sorry," he said.

"Thanks."

"There's no way I can convince you to lay low at the Brewers' place while we meet with Detective Harper?"

"Nope. I fight my own battles."

"But this isn't your—"

"It is, Noah. And I'm not giving up."

"She sounds like one of us," Michael said.

"Yeah, well she's not and she never will be," Noah countered.

The look on Rose's face made him want to take the words back, her expression a mixture of pain and anger.

"What I meant was—"

"You don't have to explain," she said.

"You're not trained like us, you can't defend yourself."

"Seems to me I have, and I've defended you as well."

"You're not cut out for this kind of violence."

"I'll have you know I took self-defense classes in Seattle and helped teach young girls how to fight off would-be attackers."

"I appreciate that, but we're talking about more than a random mugger here."

"Noah, you were the one who decided we could leave the Brewers' place and visit the nursing home. Not me."

"Yeah, Einstein," Michael interjected.

"I didn't consider someone might use social media to expose us," Noah said.

"My point is, I can take care of myself, and although I appreciate your help, and yours too, Michael, I won't be coddled or treated like a helpless child. Got it?"

"Yes," Noah said.

Michael snorted.

"That goes for you too, Michael."

"Yes, ma'am."

"We'll meet with T.J. to get a sense of what's happening, and enlist his help, then we'll make a plan to stay safe until the case is resolved with Thomas."

"That could take a while," Noah said.

Rose sighed. "You're the brilliant tech guy. Can't you prove his innocence somehow?"

"Brilliant, huh?" Michael said.

"I never said I was brilliant," Noah countered.

"Eye on the ball, guys," Rose said. "What do you need to address the current threat?"

"A laptop and VPN," Noah said.

"Beau left a laptop at the Brewer Ranch, so after our meeting with T.J. we'll head back there, and you can get to work. Then we can move on with our lives."

Move on. Right. Noah clearly heard her goal. Her priority was putting this whole experience behind her, including Noah. He represented danger and violence. No matter how much she said this was her fight too because she'd been threatened, if it hadn't been for Noah, she would be living her safe life training dogs and providing house services, helping out her family and needling her brother.

Noah's fault. All of it. Because he'd been too weak to evade his pursuers in the mountains that first day.

The day he met Rose Rogers.

"You're thinking too much," she said.

He glanced at her.

"I can tell you're sinking into that muddy, dark place. Knock it off. I need you to be sharp and focused if we're going to pull ourselves out of this."

"Nice," Michael said.

"What?" Rose said.

"I've never heard anyone challenge him like that. Good job."

"I'm still in the car," Noah said.

"But you're not torturing yourself anymore, right?" Rose said.

"No, not in this moment."

"Good, let's keep it that way."

Noah realized how well Rose knew him. After

spending only a few days in her presence, Rose had somehow tapped into his psyche and could sense his mood and interpret his thoughts. Dangerous, very dangerous.

Because Noah knew in the end he might have to make a decision she'd disagree with in order to protect her from the violence he and Thomas had brought into her life.

"And there he goes again," she said, studying him. "We're good, we're safe, let it go."

"You're bossy," he said, hoping to lighten the moment.

"Hey, bossy lady," Michael said from the front seat. "Wanna tell me where we're going?"

Rose gave him the address and Michael entered it into his navigation system.

"Whatever happens…" Noah started.

"We'll meet with T.J., figure out how to proceed legally to protect ourselves and lay low until Thomas deals with his issue. It was cowardly of him to run away and leave his friends to clean up."

"That was my choice, not his," Noah defended.

"Like it was my choice to help you, not yours. Ha!" She clapped her hands in victory.

Oscar jumped into her lap and nuzzled her ear.

"Oscar, enough." She petted him and looked at Noah. "Good, now you understand me."

Oh, he understood all right. He understood that

a strong, compassionate and caring woman sat next to him. A woman he was falling for.

A woman who deserved better than a damaged veteran like Noah.

An hour later they sat in the SUV and watched as T.J.'s sedan pulled up to the Larsons' gated estate.

Rose wished she could see inside T.J.'s car and determine if T.J. was alone or had someone in the back seat behind tinted windows. She'd warned him about Agent Hart, so he wouldn't have brought him along, but she knew he was big on having backup. She also worried that the federal agent might have followed T.J. in order to find Noah. Then there were the guys from the bridge, who were probably plenty fumed about the death of their partner Victor.

Her phone vibrated with a call.

"Hi, T.J.," she answered.

"Where are you?"

"We're close by. Watching to see if you've been followed."

"I wasn't."

"We need to be sure." She shared a look with Noah. He seemed more stoic than usual. Maybe he was still ticked that she'd taken charge before, but she had to jar him out of this self-criticism, something she recognized because she'd experienced it herself.

"You need to get yourself out of this, Rose. Now."

"You're right, I do." She glanced at Noah. "We all do. Are you alone?"

"Yes."

"We'll be there in a minute. I'll open the gates and we can meet safely on the property." She ended the call before T.J. could begin another lecture about Rose extricating herself from the situation, probably by separating herself from Noah.

She wasn't running anymore. This whole experience was teaching her to commit to a goal and stick with it to the end. She might not know what her long-term career path was, but she knew she wanted to help Noah find his friend and wouldn't give up until she saw that through. Running was not an option for Noah. The threat would continue to hound him until he was seriously injured or worse.

A cold chill rushed through her at the thought of Noah being killed by these jerks, even more tragic because he'd survived so much as a soldier in Afghanistan.

"Now who's in the mud?" Noah said.

"Guilty," she said. "Okay, what do we think? Is it safe to head down there?"

"Looks good to me." Michael pulled out of their parking spot.

"I'll press the remote to open the gates when you get close."

"Yes, ma'am."

"What was it?" Noah said.

She glanced at him.

"What were you thinking about?"

"Oh no, I've already shared way too much personal stuff with you. And it's not going to happen so…"

"What's not going to happen?"

"Bad stuff. Let's drop it, okay?" Rose tended to blurt out bold truths when nervous, and right now she was anxious about their meeting with T.J. They passed his car on the side of the road as they approached the gate.

"It's okay." Noah placed his hand over hers on the seat between them.

She glanced into his eyes and was caught there for a minute, trying to figure out why she was drawn to this man like no other in her limited dating experience.

"Excuse me, lovebirds?" Michael said from the front.

She slipped her hand from Noah's.

"Gates?"

She pressed the remote and they opened, giving them access to the circular drive.

From this vantage point she could see the entire home through the front windshield, set back amid tall trees and landscaped gardens.

"Whoa, big house," Michael said.

"Over four thousand square feet with a state-of-the-art security system."

"Then why did they hire you?" Noah asked.

"To water plants and check on things. One time they returned from vacation and the kitchen was flooded, ruining the hardwood floors. The water line to the ice maker had snapped. They hired me to hopefully prevent damage from a random event like that."

"Is this guy rich or something?" Michael said with awe in his voice.

"I guess." Money didn't impress nor intimidate Rose. People were people, whether they had millions or ten bucks in their checking account until the next pay period.

"The detective's behind us. How do we close the gates?" Michael said.

"They'll close automatically," Rose said. "Park in front. I'll get out and speak with T.J. first. Then you guys can fill him in on details while I do a walk-through."

"You're not going inside by yourself," Noah said.

"It's not dangerous, Noah. But if it'd make you feel better you guys can have your conversation inside."

They parked, and Rose got out of the car. When Oscar tried to go with, she told him to stay with Noah. She shut the door and waited for T.J. to pull up.

He frantically honked his horn as his car approached. She put out her hands in question.

"They're behind me! Get out of here!" he shouted.

"But—"

He pounded on the horn.

Noah got out of the SUV and grabbed Rose.

"Get her out of here!" T.J. shouted.

Worried about T.J., she said, "We can't leave him."

"He ordered us to leave," Noah said.

"We need to call the police, or…or…someone!"

"I'm sure he radioed for help," Noah said.

"Gates are closing," Michael said.

"Hang on." Rose hit the remote and the gates opened.

Michael peeled away from the house and through the open gates. She pressed the remote again, but the gates didn't close. That's when she spotted a security car with a flashing light on top speeding past them toward the house.

She and Noah looked out the back window.

The security car blocked the mystery car's exit. A man got out of the mystery car—one of the guys from the bridge.

He aimed a gun at the security officer.

And fired.

ELEVEN

"Michael, we need to—"

"There's a turn up ahead," Michael interrupted Noah.

"We'll jump out up there."

"Affirmative," Noah said.

"Wait, what? Who's jumping?" Rose's panic spiked. They were going to jump from a moving car?

"I'll head north," Michael said.

Noah looked at Rose. "We'll covertly exit the SUV, and they'll follow Michael thinking we're still in the vehicle," Noah said calmly.

"We're jumping? At what speed?"

"He'll slow down, but we'll have to move fast so they don't figure out he dropped us off."

"Oscar, too?"

"Oscar, too."

"But—"

Noah took her hand. "Do you trust me?"

She nodded that she did, although the words got stuck in her throat. Noah seemed calm, confident and in charge, so different from the first time they'd met in the mountains.

She sensed an understanding between him and

Michael, soldiers who had fought the enemy, soldiers who knew how to extricate themselves from a dangerous situation.

"What happens after we get out?" she said.

"We find cover."

"And then...?"

He gently squeezed her hand. She'd almost forgotten he was holding on to it.

"One move at a time, okay?" he said.

Right, of course. Because it didn't matter what they planned for after their escape unless they successfully convinced their pursuers they were still in the car.

"What about Michael?" she asked.

"I'll lead them on a crazy chase, maybe all the way to Canada. Get ready. In ten."

Rose studied Noah's expression, intent on the landscape outside Rose's window. He was probably looking for the ideal camouflage spot for temporary refuge.

She calmed her racing heart with a deep breath. She'd lectured the men about how strong she was, how independent, and said she was able to take care of herself. It was time to prove her strength and follow Noah's order when the car pulled over.

"Five," Michael said, slowing down. "When I turn up ahead, open that door."

Since Rose was on the right side of the car, she gripped the handle and readied herself for the order.

Three. Two. One.

He made the turn, pulled over and stopped.

Rose flung open the door and hopped out. Noah and Oscar practically jumped out together, Oscar having emotionally attached himself to Noah.

Noah slammed the door and pointed to a cluster of trees bordering another gated property. Holding hands, they raced toward cover.

Rose couldn't think about how close the car was, or if the men had seen their escape. She had to stay focused on hiding until the threat passed.

They scrambled into a cluster of trees, still close enough to the street to see cars drive by. Oscar danced around them, barking a few times.

"Oscar, quiet," she said.

He sat obediently and looked up at her for his next command.

"Down." She joined him by kneeling beside the tree that offered excellent cover with low-hanging limbs.

Noah motioned her to the other side of the tree trunk. She repositioned herself, and Oscar followed. Noah kneeled beside her, a slight groan rumbling against his chest. He must still be in pain from any number of physical assaults he'd survived these past few days.

Oscar made a whimpering sound. Noah reached out and stroked the dog's side. Had Oscar sensed Noah was about to have an episode? She studied Noah, but didn't get that feeling at all.

Laser-focused on the road, Noah clenched his jaw as he continued to pet Oscar.

Rose interlaced her fingers and prayed, asking the Lord for help. They needed a break from all this danger, a few hours to build their strength and figure out how they were discovered.

T.J. was the only person who knew of their plans.

No, he wouldn't have led the assailants to the Larson house. T.J. was one of the good guys.

"Okay," Noah said. "They just passed."

He looked at her, his jaw still clenched, as if he was having trouble letting go of the tension building in his body from being chased and threatened.

Oscar nudged Noah's hand because he'd stopped petting the pup. Noah didn't respond to the dog's demand for affection.

"They're gone." Rose tipped his chin so he'd look at her. "We're okay."

He blinked, lowered his gaze and started petting the dog again.

"Noah?"

He straightened. "It won't be truly okay until you're safe."

She stood and took his hand. "I am safe. Right now, with you. Because you figured out a way to protect me. What's our next move?"

He didn't answer, gazing blankly at her. It seemed like all the adrenaline to protect her had sapped his energy and his brainpower.

"I'll call Beau," she said.

"No, I don't want to involve more innocents."

"C'mon, Noah. This isn't about you putting people in danger. The men who are after you and Thomas are responsible for all this violence."

"Trust me, you would never forgive yourself if something happened to your brother because you were involved with me."

She started to argue and stopped herself, taking a minute to process his words. She finally understood how Noah felt, bringing danger into Rose's life, and why he carried so much guilt for doing so.

"Meeting with T.J. backfired on us, so I guess we're on our own," she said. "If we can get back to the Brewer Ranch, we'll be okay."

"Unless they've discovered that's our home base."

"Let's think positive."

A cocking sound echoed behind them. They both turned to see a man in his midfifties holding a rifle.

She and Noah both raised their hands. Oscar barked.

"Quiet, Oscar," she ordered, as frustration rose in her chest. Why couldn't they get a few minutes of peace?

"You're on my property," the man said.

"I'm sorry. I didn't realize it was private property," she answered, hoping that a woman responding would seem less threatening than if Noah answered, especially since it seemed like he was still in military mode.

"You can lower your hands," he said. "What are you doing here?"

"I've been hired to check on the Larson place down the road and my dog got away from me." She retrieved a business card and offered it to him.

"Rose Rogers," he said softly, and lowered his weapon. "Nick Larson mentioned you at a neighborhood get-together. You manage properties when people are away."

"Yes, sir."

"I'm Henry. Nice to meet you."

"Likewise, and this is my friend Noah Greene."

The men shook hands. Good, Noah was coming out of his zone.

"Sorry about the gun," Henry said. "I'm a bit on edge because there was a break-in up the street last month."

"I heard about that," Rose said. "A house without an alarm system, correct?"

"Yes, ma'am. Alarm systems are critical. I'm guessing that's why you brought your friend with you." He nodded at Noah.

"Yes, he makes an intimidating bodyguard. Well, I've got Oscar, so we'll be heading back to the Larson house. Nice to meet you."

"You, too."

She pulled a spare leash out of her bag and hooked it to Oscar's collar. He visibly sighed. "Let's go, buddy."

With as much confidence as she could muster, she offered Henry a smile, turned and started walking.

Two squad cars and an emergency vehicle sped past, toward the Larson place.

"We can't really go back there," Noah said softly.

"I know." The more people who saw them, the more people would know their whereabouts, exposing them to any number of enemies.

She hoped that somewhere between Henry's property and the Larson gate, they could find a safe place to hide out.

Hiding out, running from bad guys, jumping out of cars. If anyone would have told her a week ago that she'd be doing those things, she'd call them crazy. Yet here she was, in the midst of chaos, trying to manage both her and Noah's stress over remaining safe from predators.

They turned the corner and spotted three emergency vehicles parked by the gates of the Larson home.

"We need to find cover," Noah said.

"I agree." She scanned the immediate area and spotted a cluster of trees at the entrance to a gated property. "How about over here?"

A squad car suddenly pulled away from the

group of vehicles and was heading toward Noah and Rose. She wanted to seem relaxed, act like she had every right to be walking down the street with her dog and her friend. Maybe it would be more convincing…

She reached out and took Noah's hand. He glanced at her.

"We could pretend we're boyfriend and girl-friend," she said. "You know, blend into the scenery and not look so obvious?"

"I doubt you could ever blend in."

"He's probably going after the assailants, right?" she said.

"Or they're trying to find us."

As they kept looking at each other, Rose felt like a deer caught in headlights, walking along the street, an easy target.

"Maybe you should get behind me," Noah said.

She fell back slightly, but didn't let go of his hand.

The car stopped short. "Get in the car."

It was T.J. behind the wheel of the cruiser, and he looked more worried than angry. She released Noah's hand.

"You're okay," she said and reached for the car door.

Noah didn't move at first.

"Look, Noah, you saved my life," T.J. said. "Let me return the favor."

Rose nodded at Noah that it was okay, and they climbed into the back of the squad car with Oscar.

T.J. explained that the attackers rammed his car, so he couldn't pursue them, so he borrowed a squad car. Not wanting to draw attention to their safe refuge, T.J. dropped Rose, Noah and Oscar at a trailhead that was a short hike to the Brewer Ranch.

T.J. apologized for what happened at the Larson property, and said he'd speak with Mr. Larson directly to explain none of this was Rose's fault. T.J. wondered if someone in law enforcement was involved because only a few coworkers knew where he was meeting Rose and Noah.

She, Noah and Oscar hiked a half an hour to the Brewer Ranch and hesitated on the outskirts of the property.

"Everything looks normal," she said.

"Looks can be deceiving."

"No one knows we're here. We'll be fine."

Words she'd been repeating to herself throughout their mostly silent hike back to the house. It had been a stressful afternoon, eluding danger, not knowing whom to trust, and she was in desperate need of a few hours of calm.

She was also worried about Noah's mental frame of mind.

"Ready?" she said.

"Let me go first," he said.

"But—"

"I'm okay, Rose." He looked at her. "I need to do this. Let me protect you." He leaned forward, kissed her cheek and walked away.

She wondered if the sweet kiss was meant to derail her protest because it certainly worked. She held on to Oscar, even though he pulled on his leash, wanting to go with Noah.

"You've really bonded with him, haven't you, buddy?" she said.

Then again, so had Rose. Not because they were embroiled in an adrenaline-sparked relationship. Somehow, she felt like Noah was a solid partner, someone who complemented her strengths and weaknesses, and respected her opinions.

Plus, he seemed to care about her. Deeply.

"Enough," she scolded herself. This wasn't a relationship in the traditional sense of the word.

No, it was bigger than any of her previous relationships, more honest, and authentic. She didn't have to pretend with Noah, which was a new experience that made her feel safe in a different kind of way.

She wasn't always *on* or trying to please.

She was simply…herself.

Noah had seen her at her worst and her best and everything in between. Not only did he listen to her opinions, but he even let her lead when necessary. Another first.

Okay, so maybe this was what a mature relationship should look like, except without all the danger.

Oscar barked, startling her from her thoughts. She glanced across the property and saw Noah waving her over.

"Okay, go." She released Oscar and he took off running.

As she crossed the property, she silently thanked God for surviving today's events without serious injury. "To think that visiting a nursing home could be dangerous," she said. All because of a positive social media post. What would it take to stay off the radar?

By the time she reached the house, Oscar was comfortably curled up beside Noah as he sat at the kitchen table with Beau's laptop.

"You hungry?" she said, looking through the groceries the guys brought last night.

He shut the laptop. "Am I hungry?"

"It's dinnertime. The guys bought ground beef. I could make burgers."

He studied her.

"What?"

"We were almost kidnapped today, could've been seriously hurt, and you're asking if I'm hungry?"

"Well, what's the point of ruminating over what could have happened?"

"You, you are…"

"I know, I don't take direction well, I can be unfocused, scattered and—"

"Amazing." He took her hand and led her to sit beside him. "An amazing woman who's saved my life as well as any soldier could have."

"I wouldn't go that far."

"Why not?"

"I happened to be there. Thanks to God."

"I don't understand why your God threw you into this craziness."

"Because you needed me. You probably need Him, too."

Noah shook his head and withdrew his hand.

"Sorry, didn't mean to preach. But I believe He has plans for all of us. You survived horrible things in battle. You survived being injured both body and soul. But you're still here. He has things for you to do. Don't turn away from Him. 'Be still, and know that I am God.'"

She took his hand and held it securely. "I am here. God is here. We will figure this out."

"I almost believe you."

She smiled, wishing they could stay like this, seated quietly at a kitchen table, calm and at peace.

"Rose…" Noah sighed.

Was he thinking the same thing? Did he want this moment to last a bit longer to create a memory they could both hold on to in the upcoming days or even months? She had to assume he'd leave Montana, either on his own or as a witness or suspect in this case. There were so many unknowns.

Which was why she'd stay present.

Then someone knocked at the kitchen door, and she pulled her hand away from Noah's.

"Rose, are you okay? Open the door," T.J. said, trying to peek through the lace curtains.

She offered Noah a smile and let T.J. into the kitchen.

"I thought you didn't want to draw attention with the cruiser," Rose said.

"I borrowed a friend's car. No one knows where I am."

"Famous last words," Noah uttered, then glanced at T.J. "Sorry, that wasn't meant for you. We've been tracked in unexpected ways."

"Not by your phones?" T.J. asked.

"No, I deactivated location services on both our phones."

"They found us at the nursing home through social media. Can you believe that?" Rose said.

"Any word on the assailants?" Noah asked.

"Witnesses saw them speeding north." T.J.'s phone vibrated, and he glanced at it. "There was a collision on Highway 93, a black SUV."

"Michael," Noah said softly.

"Let me see what I can find out." T.J. went into the living room to make a call.

"Noah, I'm sorry," Rose said.

"Michael's tough. He'll be okay."

Now it seemed like Noah's turn to be optimistic. Or was he not accepting the alternative because it would eat away at his newly found strength?

"You're blessed to have such good friends who would do anything for you," she said.

"Yes, I am." He opened the laptop. "I'm going to do more digging, see if I can figure out how to prove Thomas is innocent."

"Let me know how I can help," she said, grabbing spices to season the burgers.

"Rose?"

She looked at him.

"You've already helped me, more than you can possibly know."

Warmth filled her chest. She continued her food preparations, feeling pleased with herself and her decisions. Life experiences could be hard, but worthwhile, and getting to know Noah and helping him during this rough time had been a good choice, no matter how foolish it may seem to others.

She realized she didn't care what others thought. For once she wasn't trying to make her parents proud or to be as clever as her siblings. She'd been called to help someone less fortunate than herself, a man whose emotional trauma affected him on a daily basis, and she'd risen to the challenge.

But it wasn't over.

"What do you hope to uncover in your research?" she asked.

"I'm trying to hack into work emails, see what the Feds are seeing that makes them so sure he's a criminal."

"And then what?"

"Prove they're forgeries or untrue I guess."

"What if…" She stopped herself, not wanting to burst his admiration of his friend.

"What if…?" he repeated.

"Never mind."

"What if he is guilty of what they're accusing him of?" Noah finished her thought.

"I shouldn't have suggested it, I'm sorry."

"Never be sorry for speaking your mind, Rose. I expect unfiltered truth from you, of all people."

She nodded.

"Yes, I've considered the possibility that my friendship has clouded my judgment of Thomas, but that won't stop me from trying to help him."

"Because you would forgive him his transgressions."

"Yes, it's in the friend contract."

"Ah, you practice forgiveness with others."

"I guess you could say that, yes."

"Then you can understand… That's what God does with you, Noah."

"My friends deserve forgiveness."

"And so do you."

T.J. reentered the kitchen, wearing a concerned frown.

"What is it?" Rose said.

"Noah's friend was taken to the hospital. Deputy says he's in good condition and should be released soon."

"Thank You, Lord," Rose said softly.

"Did he give police anything on the other car?" Noah asked.

"A description and partial plate. They've most likely switched cars by now. Who do you think the guys were at the Larson place?"

"I'd guess foreign agents," Noah said. "I suspect they shot you at the lake and one of them attacked me and Rose on the bridge."

"We retrieved the body that fell from the bridge. No ID, no wallet, nothing."

"His partners probably took it so he couldn't be traced."

"The guys at the nursing home were...?"

"Sent by Stratosphere."

"They were gone by the time sheriff's deputies arrived."

"Great, so they're still a threat," Rose said.

"Thomas should come out of hiding and put an end to all this," T.J. said.

"He'll stay hidden as long as his life is in danger and authorities consider him the enemy," Noah said.

"They must have proof of a crime or they

wouldn't be this determined to find him." T.J. sat at the table. "I'm wondering if your best move might be to turn yourself over to the Feds. Show them you have nothing to hide."

"Yeah, because that worked out so well the first time when they took me from the hospital, and I ended up unconscious on the riverbank."

"Whatever happened to the other man at the riverbank?" Rose said.

"Turned out he is, in fact, FBI. He's in the hospital recovering," T.J. said.

"And Agent Hart?" Noah said. "Have you contacted his superiors about the orderly being threatened? They couldn't have approved that."

"I was working on tracking down Hart's supervisor when I got your call to meet at the Larson property," T.J. said.

Rose watched the interchange, relieved that the two men had finally come to a truce and were working together. She respected both of them and knew once they combined their knowledge and intellect, the situation would improve.

Oscar's ears pricked and he rushed to the front of the house, frantically barking.

"That's probably Adam checking in." Rose left the kitchen.

"Rose, wait," Noah said.

The front door burst open.

The two Stratosphere agents stormed into the living room, guns drawn.

TWELVE

The detective put out his hand for Noah to stay back.

Noah could barely stop himself from rushing out there and protecting Rose. Exposing himself would serve no purpose other than making himself a target. Yet he couldn't stand the thought of them hurting Rose.

"We've got your friend," one of the guys called out. "Come with us and we'll let her go."

Oscar continued to bark his protest.

The detective motioned with his hand that he was going out the back door and would circle around the front. Noah nodded his approval of the plan. The guys knew Noah was in the house, but not the detective, so the element of surprise could work in their favor.

"Shut that dog up or I will," another guy said.

Noah fisted his hand. They'd hurt a dog? Cowards.

"Oscar, quiet," Rose said.

The dog quieted for a minute, then started barking again. A good distraction in a way, but Noah didn't want them to hurt Oscar, especially in front of Rose.

Noah stood, readying himself for whatever was to come next.

Whatever would stop them from hurting Rose.

"C'mon out, Greene!"

He took a deep breath and considered his options. If he stayed hidden, they might turn aggressive. By now the detective must be close to the front door. If Noah stepped into the living room and distracted them, the detective could attack from behind.

"Did you hear me?" the guy said.

"I heard you." Noah stepped into the doorway, hands raised. The two Stratosphere agents stood in the living room, not far from the front door, one with a firm grip of Rose's arm.

"Ah, there he is," the taller guy said.

Oscar's barking intensified, as if he knew not only Rose, but also Noah was in danger.

"Shut up!" the shorter agent shouted at Oscar. Then aimed his gun at the dog.

"Oscar, quiet," Noah ordered.

The dog stopped barking and looked at Noah, but stayed near Rose.

"Okay, you've got me. I'll go willingly, so you can release Rose."

"We'll let her go when you're in the car heading back to Virginia with us," the shorter guy said.

"Fine. Let's go."

"Noah, don't," Rose said.

"Quiet, Rose."

"Listen to your boyfriend." The taller guy shoved Rose into the sofa.

Oscar started barking again.

"Shut up!" The tall one aimed his gun at the dog.

"No!" Rose scrambled to Oscar and shielded him in her arms.

The detective burst through the front door and grabbed the shorter guy from behind.

As the Stratosphere goon struggled to free himself, the gun went off, a bullet hitting the china cabinet.

The tall guy spun around to help his friend, and Noah launched himself across the room, tackling him and dislodging his gun. It hit the ground. Noah focused on keeping the guy away from the weapon.

He punched and shoved, and did everything in his power to neutralize the tall guy. They were equally matched, but Noah had one extra thing going for him: his intense feelings for Rose. He would kill to protect her if necessary. Noah got his hands around the tall guy's neck and squeezed.

The guy slammed his fist into Noah's injured ribs, and he hissed against the pain, but didn't give up his hold of the guy's neck. Noah heard a thud and moan.

"Enough!" Rose shouted.

The tall guy froze. Noah looked up and saw Rose aiming the guy's gun at his head.

"Pops taught me never to aim a gun at something unless I planned to destroy it."

The tall guy didn't move.

"I won't have a problem pulling the trigger," she said.

Oscar barked as if making her point clear.

"Grover?" the tall guy said.

"He can't help you." The detective pulled the tall guy's hands behind his back and cuffed him. He pulled him off Noah and shoved him face-down on the floor. Harper read him his rights and motioned to Rose, who passed him the assailant's gun.

Oscar ran up to Noah and nuzzled his cheek.

"Oscar, leave it," Rose said.

"It's okay." Noah sat up and stroked the dog's fur. "I'm okay, buddy."

"I'll call for a unit to take these guys to lockup," the detective said.

"That will expose our location," Rose protested.

Noah and the detective shared a look.

"We've already been exposed," Noah said.

"Oh. So, now what?" Rose said.

"We need to secure that one." Detective Harper nodded at the unconscious man on the floor. "Rose, find me some rope, or string?"

"Sure." She dashed off into the kitchen.

Noah pieced together what just happened: Rose clobbered the now-unconscious guy with a lamp to stun him, giving the detective an advantage, then she grabbed the taller guy's gun off the floor. She had saved Noah's and the detective's lives.

She was, in a word, remarkable.

Rose returned from the kitchen with a spool of twine. "Will this work?"

"Yeah, great." The detective secured the unconscious guy's hands behind his back.

The tall guy who'd been on top of Noah tried to turn over. Noah placed his boot on the assailant's back. "That's not happening."

"Let's take him outside so we don't cause any more damage in here," the detective said.

Noah and Detective Harper pulled the tall guy to his feet and escorted him to the front porch, and into a chair. The detective passed Noah the twine to secure him, and went back inside for the other guy. Noah wrapped twine around the guy's arms and torso, securing him to the chair.

Noah was done running from these guys, and wanted to eliminate them from the equation.

The detective dragged the unconscious man out onto the porch, Noah tossed him the twine and the detective secured him to the porch railing.

"These guys are affiliated with Stratosphere?" Harper asked, hovering over the one in the chair.

"Yes, sir," Noah said, as Rose stood on the porch with Oscar by her side. "Stratosphere is the company I work for that developed the software the Feds think my friend is selling to foreign agents."

"Think? They know. We all know he's making a deal for millions of dollars," the tall guy said, glaring at Noah. "Even if you deny it."

"What proof do you have?" Noah said.

"Video evidence of Thomas Young meeting with foreign agents."

"Video can be manipulated," Noah defended.

"Phone calls, emails, recorded conversations."

"And you were sent to find Thomas and Noah in order to what?" Harper asked.

The guy didn't answer.

"If they'd wanted me dead, they've had plenty of opportunity," Noah said.

"Then they want you back at work? Why?" the detective asked.

"A company like Stratosphere only cares about the bottom line," Noah said. "If word leaks that they can't control their own employees, that their employees are making deals with foreign agents, which we're not, their stock will plummet. Then again, there's another possibility."

"What's that?" Harper said.

"Stratosphere could have made a deal with the Feds to retrieve Thomas and hand him over in exchange for not holding Stratosphere responsible for their part in this crime."

"The company is not responsible for your friend's criminal activity," the tall guy said.

"Companies have some culpability in regard to their employees, but it looks like Stratosphere is diverting the entire blame onto Thomas," Noah said.

"If Stratosphere has proof and turned it over to the Feds, then case closed on your friend, I'm afraid," Harper said.

Noah fisted his hand. "Thomas is not an enemy of the state. He is a decorated soldier."

"I believe you, but running makes him look guilty," Harper said. "Coming out of hiding and facing his accusers is the only way to clear his name."

"My friends went to find him and convince him to come back," Noah said.

"Any luck so far?"

"I haven't heard that they've found him."

"I'd better call for backup and alert federal authorities about our friends here. Once I do, they'll most likely want to take you into custody as well, to help with their case against Thomas."

"I don't trust the Feds," Noah said.

"I understand, but I'm not sure you have much choice. Even with these Stratosphere guys in custody, the Feds and foreign agents are still after you, right?" He glanced at Rose with a worried frown.

"I need more time before I'm locked up for a crime I didn't commit," Noah said.

"Hey, it's not my place to tell you what to do, as long as you consider Rose's safety."

"That's my primary concern."

"I'm taking you at your word. But I think Rose should stay here with me."

"I agree," Noah said.

"Rose is going with Noah, thank-you-very-much," she said. "I still have a target on my back and I'd feel safer in the wilderness than anywhere else."

"I'm assuming I can't talk you out of that decision?" Harper said.

"Good assumption."

Noah didn't even try to dissuade her from coming with him. He knew he'd lose that argument. "We can head into the mountains and meet up with my buddies."

The detective put up his hand. "I don't want to know your plans. I'm calling for backup. Do what you need to do."

"Won't you get in trouble if we're not here when they arrive?" Rose said.

"I'll figure it out." He pinned Noah with a serious look.

"Don't worry, I'll take care of Rose," Noah said.

"Make sure you do."

An hour later, Rose and Noah were on a trail heading north into the mountains. Oscar trotted ahead of them, as if sniffing out danger. Or maybe that was hopeful thinking on Rose's part.

"You're quiet," Noah said.

"Tired I guess." And pensive, and worried. Worried about T.J. getting in trouble because he was giving her and Noah a head start. Worried that rumors about Rose and Noah might swirl around town, and what Mom and Dad would think if those rumors landed at the ranch.

Then she caught herself. She was a grown woman and shouldn't care what other people thought of her relationship with Noah. She certainly was able to make good choices and decisions.

Staying off the grid for another twenty-four hours was the best decision going forward. She certainly didn't want to wait around for the next attack. It was best to keep moving and stay on the offensive.

"We could pitch camp soon if you want," Noah said.

"Then what?"

"Hook up with Chris and Willy, hopefully later tonight or early tomorrow."

"I thought they were looking for Thomas."

"They're taking a break to help me protect you."

"But finding Thomas is the key to resolving all this," she said.

"True."

"Then we shouldn't distract them from their goal."

"Keeping you safe is our priority."

"I don't like that you're abandoning the mission because of me."

"We're not abandoning it. We're pressing Pause for a day."

She sighed and shook her head.

"This whole thing will eventually end, you know," he said.

He sounded confident, self-assured. She'd like to think being around her and Oscar these past few days had helped him somehow. She hoped so, anyway.

The prospect of this danger ending gave her peace, but it also caused a wave of melancholy at the thought of never seeing Noah again. He was one of the few people she'd been brutally honest with, and it felt good, like a pressure valve had been released and she could finally breathe.

"Where's Cathy?" he said.

She looked at him. "Who?"

"Chatty Cathy? You know, the one that always has something interesting to say."

"I don't know about interesting."

"I do. Come on, what's bugging you? Did you want to stay back at the Brewer place with the detective?"

"No. I need to see this through to the end, complete something for a change instead of running away when things get hard."

"Oh, and here I thought you liked my company," he joked.

"I *do* like your company, Noah. That's the problem."

"I don't understand."

"I enjoy talking to you, hiking in nature with you. But this isn't a normal relationship. Are these feelings even real? Or am I making more bad decisions because that's in my DNA?"

He didn't respond, and she thought she might have offended him.

"Oh, don't take it personally," she said. "I was grappling with some heady life questions when I discovered you the other day, and our friendship has forced me to finally accept some hard truths."

"I'm sorry if I've caused you pain."

"No, no." She stopped and touched his arm. "You didn't do anything like that. As a matter of fact, you've challenged me to acknowledge things I may not have admitted before. You're not allowed to carry responsibility for my issues."

"I understand. But I feel responsible for you, Rose."

"I get it." She continued walking, disappointed.

Like everyone else, he felt responsible for Rosie because he didn't think she could take care of herself. And here she thought she'd developed a connection with someone who recognized her strengths, her determination. He'd said as much, right?

"What do you get, Rose?" Noah asked, studying her.

"I appreciate you wanting to protect me because, well, I can't manage on my own."

"Hang on, weren't you the one preaching to me about accepting help from others?"

"Helping a friend is one thing. This, what you're doing, is different."

"Explain?"

"I've helped you a few times, so naturally you feel responsible for me. It's fine." She waved him off.

"I feel responsible because I care about you," he said.

"You care because you're grateful for my help. It's okay, I understand."

"It's more than that. I care because I admire your selflessness, your strength, your sense of humor… Your commitment to helping others—"

"You mean like when I found you?"

"Not just me, but how you take care of people's homes, giving them peace of mind. How you help out your family, and took Oscar to the nursing home."

"Some people think that's just me being unable to commit to any one thing, scattered and all over the place."

"Those people are wrong. What you do is important on a deeper level than a typical job. I do a job, I get a paycheck. Done. But you... I wasn't in the nursing home, but I'll bet you brought joy to the seniors when you introduced them to Oscar."

The image of an elderly woman's face lighting up flashed across her thoughts, followed by a man's peaceful smile when he stroked Oscar's soft fur.

"You are taking care of the Brewers' house so they can enjoy their time away—"

"Bad example since I broke a lamp and there's a bullet hole in their china cabinet."

"They will understand that bigger things are at play here, things out of your control. My point is, you're a generous and strong person who offers her talents to make others' lives easier and better. Not many people can or choose to do that. It's a true gift, and I admire you for it."

They walked a few minutes in silence. She wasn't sure what to do with his praise, struggling to accept the truth to his words.

Generous, sure. Rose loved helping others, making their lives easier, better.

But strong? He'd called her strong. She'd never thought of herself that way. Well, maybe not until recently. Briefly remembering the multiple times in the past few days she'd helped Noah, evaded danger, outwitted their attackers, she caught herself standing a little taller. It's like he'd held up a mirror for Rose to truly see herself as she was, not as she thought others saw her.

How was that possible?

"I'm sorry. I've upset you," he said.

"I'm not upset. I'm processing. Sometimes it takes a few minutes for everything to compute."

"Can I help?"

"Not right now, thanks." She adjusted the backpack she'd borrowed from the Brewers' place across her shoulders and forged ahead. Rose needed time to analyze her own thoughts and feelings, time to pray and ask for God's guidance.

She felt Noah's hand on her shoulder and she hesitated, turning to him.

"Never question your feelings, Rose. Trust them, believe in them. They could save your life."

A few hours later they were about to pitch camp when Noah got a message from Willy. Closing in on what they thought was Thomas's location, they actually weren't far from Noah and Rose. Noah was relieved they'd meet up sooner rather than later. Willy asked if Noah and Rose could hike a bit longer to rendezvous with the guys.

Noah let Rose make the decision. Although he might be anxious to connect with Thomas, Noah's priority was Rose's well-being. If she felt too tired to continue, they would pitch camp.

Rose said they should keep going. Noah figured Thomas represented the end of the danger that had been hounding her since she'd found him and selflessly decided to help.

"Good timing to meet up with the guys when they're about to find Thomas," she said.

"Very good timing."

"My prayers must have worked." She glanced over her shoulder and winked.

That playful and pleased expression would be seared into his memory forever. An expression born of her faith in God.

"It's okay if you don't agree with me." She continued up the trail.

"Actually, I'd like to agree with you. I'm… warming up to the idea that prayer can actually have an impact on my life."

"Good, then if nothing else, your time spent with me has opened your heart to the wonder of faith."

His heart surely had been opened to faith, and much more where Rose was concerned. Through her eyes, he'd seen how helping someone was a loving act for both the person being helped and the person doing the helping. The way Rose's face practically glowed when they went to the nursing home to bring joy to complete strangers made Noah rethink his aversion to being helped. He'd felt beholden to Thomas after he'd saved Noah's life, so much so, Noah had risked his own life to come to Montana to find and help his friend.

Yet Thomas had told him to go home. He didn't

want Noah's help. Perhaps like Noah didn't want to put Rose in danger, Thomas didn't want Noah in the line of fire either.

Or was it something else? Did Thomas fear Noah would be painted with the same brush, be branded a traitor who betrayed his country?

No, Noah was confident they would find Thomas and clear his name, prove his innocence, and life would go back to normal.

Normal. Without Rose.

A wave of sadness rolled through his chest. He would miss her bright, loving energy, realizing how mundane his life had been before he'd met Rose. Doing the same thing every day without inspiration or passion. Yet Rose was inspired by many things, and it was contagious. Her dog, the wilderness, her business and her family. Even though she sometimes struggled with her place in the Rogers family, he could sense her unconditional love and affection for them, especially her protective big brother.

The image of Noah being welcomed at the Rogers family dinner table sparked across his thoughts. What a life that would be...

He reprimanded himself. He had to focus on keeping Rose safe, not get distracted by the image of what could never be, or the grief sure to swallow him whole once he left Montana and lost his connection to the spirited and hopeful woman.

"Hey, there's a cabin over there. Could that be it?" Rose said.

He studied the cabin in the distance on the other side of the river. "Coordinates are right."

"We'll have to hike down, and then cross the river."

"Lead on," he said.

She seemed to like being in charge, having control over her situation. Made total sense. She'd mostly been fleeing a cunning enemy who knew where they'd be before they got there, an enemy who wasn't even hers.

As he followed her determined pace, he admired her ability to stay strong and continue on their quest without complaint. He wasn't so sure he would have been so accepting if roles were reversed.

"Do you see Willy and Chris anywhere?" she said.

He hesitated and pulled out binoculars he'd borrowed from the Brewers' place to scan the area. There was a light in the cabin, which gave him hope Thomas was inside, but he saw no sign of Willy or Chris.

They picked up speed as they headed down to cross the river.

"Watch your step!" he called after her.

A few hairpin turns later and they'd made it to the riverbank.

"Look!" She pointed across the river at a man approaching the cabin.

"Thomas?" Noah whispered. "Thomas!" He waved.

Thomas hesitated and looked toward Noah and Rose but didn't seem to see them.

"Over here!" Noah shouted.

Thomas turned his back on them and went into the cabin.

Noah pulled out his phone and called Willy. "Are you guys close? He's here, we saw him at the cabin."

"Noah!" Rose said.

The two guys from the bridge approached the cabin.

"No," Noah ground out. "Thomas!" he called although it was futile because Thomas couldn't hear him.

But the assailants did.

One of them whipped out a gun and fired. Noah grabbed Rose and pulled her to the ground, shielding her with his own body. The guy, who Noah suspected was a foreign agent, got off another few rounds, one bullet hitting the ground beside them.

"Stay down," he ordered Rose.

Two more shots were fired; then silence.

Noah peered across the river. The guys were out of sight, probably refocused on their primary target: Thomas.

Noah had to move fast if he was going to help his friend.

"Rose, we're clear," he said.

She didn't respond.

"Rose?"

He turned her over. Her eyes were closed, and her skin pale. He pulled his hand away.

It was smeared with blood.

THIRTEEN

Noah couldn't breathe.

He had to... He had to do something. Had to save Rose.

Yet he couldn't even move, paralyzed by the memory of...

He was back there. In the sandbox.

Then someone leaned against him, bringing him back from the edge, offering support, hope.

Not someone. Some*thing*.

Oscar.

Noah was looking into the dog's expectant brown eyes.

Something snapped inside Noah's chest. He shook off the memory and focused on the situation at hand.

Rose.

"Rose, can you hear me?" He guided his hands up and down her arms, then her torso, looking for a bullet wound, but found none.

Oscar whined.

"C'mon, sweetheart, open your eyes. I can't... lose you."

As if feeling the same way, Oscar nuzzled Rose's ear, desperate for her to awaken.

"Uh…" she said. "Oscar, stop."

Oscar kept nuzzling, and she gently batted him away. "I'm okay, I'm okay."

Noah swiped at his own watery eyes.

"You know how I hate the ear stuff." She blinked her beautiful green eyes open and looked at Noah. "What happened? Is Thomas okay?"

"I… I don't know."

Rose sat up and groaned. "Whoa, I think I hit my head when I went down."

He noticed a laceration on the side of her head. "Take it easy."

Gunfire echoed through the mountains.

Noah ducked and shielded Rose. He looked across the river. Thomas had knocked one guy out and was struggling to get the gun away from the other one.

"Go help him," Rose ordered.

He couldn't bring himself to leave.

"Don't you dare stay back because of me, Noah."

He started to get up and spotted Willy and Chris coming down the trail. Relief coursed through him. Good timing. They'd help.

Noah wouldn't have to leave Rose behind.

Thomas and the gunman hit the ground and rolled toward the river. The gun flew out of the assailant's hand.

Willy and Chris were close…

Thomas scrambled to his feet and went for the gun.

The attacker pulled a second gun and shouted something. Thomas froze, raising his hands.

Turned to his attacker.

The irrational part of Noah wanted to take off running, to get there before Thomas was shot and killed, but Noah knew it was impossible to reach him in time.

"C'mon, Willy," Noah muttered.

"They need him alive, right? They won't shoot him," Rose said.

Something distracted the gunman.

Thomas grabbed the other gun, spun around and aimed—

The gunman fired twice.

Thomas stumbled, clutching his chest.

"No!" Noah shouted.

Thomas fell into the river.

Willy tackled the gunman, and Chris rushed to the riverbank to track Thomas.

But instead of following the river's current, Chris froze and raised his hands. Four men with assault rifles approached them from behind.

Noah recognized Agent Hart.

"Feds," he said.

"Forget them, and go find Thomas," Rose said.

"You'll be—"

"I'm fine, go!"

Noah took off, jogging along the riverbank,

trying to spot any sign of Thomas's black jacket floating on the water's surface.

He saw nothing. No sign of his friend struggling to stay afloat. Which meant what? He'd drowned? No, Noah wouldn't accept that.

The riverbank all but disappeared, forcing Noah to go into the water to continue his quest to find Thomas. He clenched his jaw against the chill, wading up to his thighs.

The flow increased in speed, as if…

And then he saw it in the distance—a drop-off to a waterfall.

"No," he ground out, trying to move faster.

His foot slipped and he went down, dropping beneath the water's surface. The current caught hold of him, and he fought against it, struggled to stand, but couldn't get solid footing. He flailed his arms, reaching for something to stop the momentum. He finally caught a tree limb that had fallen into the river, and he took a deep breath.

He looked up just as Thomas's jacket drifted over the edge and disappeared into the waterfall.

"Thomas," he said softly. "Thomas, I'm sorry."

Back at Thomas's cabin, Rose, Noah, Willy and Chris were waiting to be officially questioned.

Rose didn't like the way Noah looked, his skin pale, his expression beyond blank. His clothes were damp, and he should be fighting off hypothermia, but he didn't seem to feel anything.

At all.

When she'd touched his cheek a few minutes ago, he simply stared straight ahead. Even Oscar couldn't bring him around.

Rose, Noah and his friends sat around a cabin fire, built to keep them all warm, especially Noah.

She wished they could hike back to town, but federal agents were threatening them with criminal charges if they didn't follow procedure, stick around and give statements.

The door opened and Agent Hart entered. He slid a chair in front of Noah.

Rose pursed her lips to keep from saying something snappy. She didn't trust this man, and wanted to get between them to defend Noah, to protect him since he was in such a vulnerable state right now.

Oh sure, like she could defend him from four federal agents?

"I'm sorry," Agent Hart said. "They've found Thomas's body."

Rose touched Noah's shoulder. *Give him comfort, Lord.*

Noah sighed deeply.

"God bless, my friend," Willy said softly.

Chris muttered something inaudible.

"I'm also sorry that I handled this case so… well, unprofessionally," Agent Hart said. "My orders were to do whatever was necessary to prevent foreign enemies from trying to destroy our country through a cyberattack. My partner is young and overzealous. He only knew we had to find Thomas, not that Thomas was working with me."

"Working with you?" Noah said.

"Yes, he was a whistleblower."

"Why should I believe anything you say?" Noah countered.

"I understand your resentment. It's well deserved."

The agent's response surprised Rose.

"I'd like to share some information to help you see the whole picture," Agent Hart started. "This is confidential, but I think necessary for you to understand what's been going on."

Noah just stared into the fire.

"Continue," Willy said.

"Thomas discovered suspicious activity at Stratosphere and anonymously contacted my department to report it. He was smart, your friend. He encrypted all communication so no one could track the source and come after him, especially the Russians."

"If he was smart, he would still be alive," Noah said, bitterly.

Anger, resentment, grief. Rose read all three on his face and wanted to ease his pain.

"So, it was the Russians," Willy said.

"Yes," Hart confirmed. "Thomas was gathering intel about Stratosphere developing code to sell to the Russians. Our goal was to bring both to justice. We think Stratosphere suspected what he was doing, and they shut down the deal."

"Then why were Stratosphere agents after Thomas?" Rose asked.

"To bring him back, find out how much he knew," Agent Hart said. "Frustrated that Stratosphere pulled out before he could get everything he needed, Thomas decided to lure the Russians out on his own."

"And you let him do that?" Noah said.

"I discouraged his plan, but he was going forward with or without my approval. To protect his cover, and convince the Russians Thomas was a legitimate player, we acted as if we wanted to find and arrest Thomas. Only myself and my supervisor were privy to this plan. If the Russians discovered the truth, I feared they'd kill him. When he disappeared, I thought that's what happened, but then I received a message explaining he'd gone to Montana to lay low." Agent Hart sighed. "Noah, I'm sorry if I seemed aggressive when questioning you at the hospital. I was worried about Thomas's safety and wanted to find him ASAP. Even though my partner didn't know the full story, he shouldn't have threatened the orderly the way he did."

"Ya think?" Chris said.

"Not helping," Willy scolded.

"In his defense, all Smitty knew was that

Thomas was working with foreign enemies. However, that's no excuse for his behavior and he has been suspended," Agent Hart said.

"Thomas was never guilty of anything," Rose said.

"Except putting himself in danger to protect our country," Willy said.

"Secrecy was key. Until today," Agent Hart said. "He contacted me and asked that we bring him in and officially charge him in order to get the Russian agents to leave his friends alone."

"He's dead because of me," Noah said flatly.

"You didn't shoot him," Rose said.

"True, that," Chris agreed.

"If he'd only told me what was going on…" Noah said.

"He didn't want to make you a target," Agent Hart said.

"No, I did that all by myself," Noah said.

"What happened to the shooter?" Willy pressed.

"My men took the Russians in for questioning."

"But you're keeping us here," Noah said.

"We thought it best to keep you guys away from them."

Willy and Chris shared a look. "Probably right," Willy said.

"If the Russians thought Thomas was working with them, why shoot him?" Chris said.

"It was self-defense," Noah offered. "Thomas was about to shoot the guy."

"But Thomas wasn't fast enough," Chris said softly.

Silence permeated the cabin.

"What happens now?" Rose asked Agent Hart.

"I could use Noah's help going through Thomas's encrypted files to finish building our case against Stratosphere," the agent said.

"Don't you have forensic experts for that?" Noah said.

"Yes, but they don't know Thomas like you do."

Noah didn't respond. The room grew quiet.

Rose thought this might be his opportunity to find closure around Thomas's death. Closure certainly would have helped Rose process the loss of her sister.

She placed her hand on Noah's shoulder. "What would Thomas want you to do?"

He shot her an indignant look, but she didn't pull away. She knew he wasn't angry with her, that the anger was directed at his friend, for both not trusting Noah with the truth and for abandoning him.

"We continue, even if our brothers have fallen," Willy said.

Noah blinked, a hint of acceptance coloring his blue eyes. "I'll help." He glanced at Agent Hart. "What about the Russians?"

"We'll get them, too. The sooner we build the case against everyone involved, the sooner you can get back to your lives."

* * *

They left the cabin early the next morning and made it down by eleven. Noah convinced Agent Hart to let him work from the Brewer Ranch using Beau's computer, and the agent agreed, which surprised Rose.

She liked the thought of having Noah and his friends close by, and Mr. Brewer wholeheartedly approved of his residence being used as a home base for a federal investigation. Willy even spoke to Mr. Brewer by phone to thank him for his generosity.

Things were falling into place, even though Rose felt a little off-kilter. She wasn't nervous about the potential danger, since Willy and Chris, plus federal agents at the ranch, would keep everyone safe.

Something else bothered her. Maybe that this all felt normal, comfortable.

This wasn't reality, she kept reminding herself.

She went upstairs to check on Noah, who was working in a guest bedroom for privacy. She tapped on the door, but there was no response.

"Noah? Brought you coffee." She pushed open the door with her foot.

Noah was staring out the window.

She placed the mug of coffee on the desk beside the laptop. "How's it going?"

He didn't answer.

She went to the window to see what he was

looking at. Willy and Chris were chatting with Adam about the horse he was exercising in the pen. Adam motioned for Chris to grab a saddle off the fence and the two men put it on the horse. "Oh boy, riding lessons."

She turned to Noah, who seemed lost.

"Noah?"

"Why didn't he trust me enough to tell me what was going on? I could have helped. Maybe he'd still be alive."

She kneeled and touched his hand, resting on his thigh. "He was protecting you."

"Right, because I was too weak and fragile to be an asset to him."

"No, because he cared about you."

"If you care about someone, you're honest. You trust them with your thoughts, and you include them in your decisions."

"He must have had his reasons."

"I feel like I've failed him somehow. If I'd been a better friend, a stronger man…"

"Don't talk like that. I don't know anyone who would drop everything like you did and travel across the country because you thought Thomas was in trouble. You're a loyal and remarkable man."

"Who couldn't save his friend."

"Listen, Thomas made his own decisions, decisions that put him in danger. He knew the risks but felt it necessary to do what was right for his country, and his friends. Once he knew you were in danger, he called in reinforcements, Willy, Chris and Michael. Speaking of which, Agent Hart said Michael is on his way back here."

He nodded. "That's good."

"Hey." She touched his cheek. "I'm so sorry about Thomas. You must take your time grieving for him, but in the meantime don't give up on the rest of us, on trusting people, because Thomas chose to protect you and keep you in the dark."

"Rose, I could never give up on you."

"That's… That's a very nice thing to say."

"I mean it."

The intensity of his expression made her feel exposed somehow, like he saw through her protective shell and understood the subtext of her words: she'd almost given up on herself a few times but managed to keep going with the help of her faith.

To think what her life would look like with the support of a man like Noah, someone who respected her, believed in her. She couldn't help but smile.

"What?" he said.

"Not to be weird or anything, but I was thinking what a blessing it was that we ran into each other the way we did."

"Even after everything that's happened? You call that a blessing?"

"I do. I've never known anyone like you, Noah. I hope we're friends for a long time."

"Friends," he said, flatly.

"Sure, friendship is always a good place to start. And then, well, who knows where we might end up. I'm open to the possibilities." She planted a kiss on his cheek and left the room, hoping she wasn't being too forward.

But she needed him to know how she felt, that she would be seriously interested in a future together once things settled down.

So, now he knew. The rest was up to him.

Staring at the doorway, Noah touched his cheek and realized he was smiling. Rose was right, friendship was a good place to start. It also sounded like she was open to more than simple friendship.

She understood him and was able to help him process his dark mood. His intense emotions were driven by guilt and grief. It would take time to deal with both. He was angry with Thomas, but still loved him as a friend. The least he could do was finish what Thomas started.

Gathering evidence that got Thomas killed.

That almost got Rose killed.

When Noah thought Rose had been shot and seriously wounded, his heart felt as if it was being crushed by a twelve-ton weight. It was like all the energy in his body had evaporated, leaving an empty shell.

That's when he realized he'd fallen in love with her.

"Can't deal with that right now," he muttered, because he couldn't. He didn't have the bandwidth to consider what he should do with these heady, wonderful emotions, while navigating the darker ones of grief and despair.

Besides, it wasn't fair to express his truth given how they'd met. This wasn't a real relationship, was it? They hadn't dated, emailed or texted like people do when they're interested in romance.

No, but they'd spent nearly a week together, eluding danger while sharing vulnerabilities, fears and hopes. It was a relationship so different from any others he'd experienced.

Stronger, deeper and somehow more comfortable. More…authentic.

Oscar rushed into the room, disrupting Noah's train of thought.

"Hey, buddy. I wondered where you've been." He ruffled the dog's fur and studied his own hand, realizing how much had changed. He'd been afraid of dogs before he'd met Oscar and yet now he smiled every time Oscar came to greet him.

And when Rose entered the room…

If this was real, if he wanted to pursue a long-lasting relationship with Rose, he'd have to finish helping the Feds first.

As he surfed through Thomas's cloud drive, a folder named "Friends" popped up. He clicked it open to reveal photos of Thomas, Noah and the guys. It comforted Noah to see Thomas's goofy smile. Then he clicked on a video file of the guys playing football at a park near Thomas's apartment, one of the few times they got together stateside.

Noah found himself smiling as he watched Thomas intercept a pass meant for Michael. Thomas ran it in for a touchdown, and Noah rushed over to slap a high five.

"Let's celebrate!" Thomas called out to the guys.

"You won, we lost," Michael countered. Chris and Willy approached.

"We all won," Thomas said. "We made it back alive. Friends till the end, and beyond!"

They slapped high fives and the video ended.

"Friends till the end, and beyond," Noah said softly, leaning back in his chair.

Noah must finish his friend's good work.

He refocused on digging through Thomas's files, hoping to find more evidence to bring Stratosphere and the Russians to justice. As he went deeper into his friend's cloud account, Noah realized Thomas had hacked into his Russian contact's email and text messaging using a program

Thomas had designed that automatically updated new files. Noah clicked on a file containing information about the Russians' plans. Thomas had gathered a lot of evidence implicating the Russians.

Noah clicked on another folder, and multiple images popped onto the screen.

Of Montana, of Noah.

And Rose.

Rose at her family's ranch. Rose at a dog training session.

Rose laughing.

The photographer was so close that Noah could see the twinkle in her eye.

It sent a chill down his spine.

Another image popped up of Rose with a text message: Find her.

Noah leaned back in his chair. What did they want with Rose?

He checked the date of the text: it was sent *after* Thomas had been shot. Surely after Thomas's death the Russians would have no reason to *find* Rose. Plus, the Russians were in lockup. They weren't a threat.

Oscar's ears pricked as pounding echoed from the stairs. Chris slid into the doorway. "The Russians broke out of custody while being transferred."

"Where's Rose?"

"Downstairs on the phone."

"What are the Feds planning to do?"

"They aren't sharing. Willy and I are strategizing. Michael should be here soon. Come downstairs."

"Gotta finish something first."

Chris disappeared from the doorway.

If Russian agents could break out of custody, they could pretty much do anything.

Like kidnap an innocent young woman.

No, that didn't make sense. Why would they be after Rose?

It didn't matter. He couldn't risk it.

Noah couldn't stand the thought of her being in danger, being hurt because Noah had come to Montana to find Thomas.

Noah couldn't save his friend.

But he *could* save Rose.

It was time to stop being the traumatized soldier who couldn't protect the people he loved.

He turned back to the computer and fired off an email and text message to the Russian contact: I've got what you want. Let's meet.

He didn't care that this was a dangerous move, one that could end his life. The only thing that mattered was protecting Rose.

The flurry of activity at the ranch made Rose nervous. She wished Noah would come downstairs and join his friends, who brainstormed ways to keep everyone safe, especially the civilians who'd been pulled into this mess.

Rose heard the subtext in the conversation among the veterans: they were all trying to protect Rose.

They sensed she meant a lot to Noah, Willy commenting how Noah seemed better than he had in a long time. Better, more like himself, more at peace.

That could be true, but it was also true that she, herself, felt more grounded and at peace when she was with Noah. She'd surprised herself when she kissed him on the cheek, but it felt like a natural expression of how she felt and she wanted him to know, without a doubt, she was open to more than friendship.

It had been half an hour since the kiss, and he was still hiding upstairs.

He's not hiding, he's working, trying to find answers in order to protect you.

In any case, his absence was making her antsy. Not good. There was no guarantee his feelings were as strong for Rose as hers were for him. More importantly, were they strong enough to inspire him to move to Montana from Virginia?

Montana? Was Rose seriously considering staying after this was over? What about her city-girl life in Seattle?

Okay, the last week must be getting to her because she was all over the place right now.

Willy glanced through the window. "Something's up."

Rose followed his gaze and saw two sheriff's deputies out back talking with two federal agents.

"I'll check it out. Stay here," Willy said, and went outside.

"I'm going to check on Noah," Rose said.

"Yeah, maybe he'll listen to you and grace us with his presence," Chris said.

"Noah doesn't listen to anyone, you know that," Michael countered.

The men continued to banter back and forth as she headed through the living room toward the stairs. She smiled to herself, realizing this felt like a family, the three veterans and Rose.

As she reached the top of the stairs, she wondered if Oscar was in the bedroom with Noah. She hadn't seen him in a while and assumed as much.

The door was shut. She hesitated and knocked.

"Hey, Noah? We could use your help downstairs," she tried.

When there was no response, she opened the door.

The room was empty.

FOURTEEN

Rose rushed down the stairs to the kitchen. "He's not there, he's not in the bedroom."

Chris opened the back door. "Willy!"

Michael and Chris shared a look of concern. Willy entered the kitchen.

"Noah's gone," Chris said.

Willy shut the back door. "I know."

"You know? Where did he go?" Rose said.

"To meet with the Russian agents."

"What? That's not his responsibility," Rose said.

"Apparently he felt it was. He didn't tell the Feds what he was planning until after he was gone."

"They would have tried to stop him," Chris said.

"They would have tried," Michael offered.

"Agent Hart and his team are tracking Noah," Willy said. "They're hoping he'll get the final evidence they need to bring charges against the Russians."

"Agent Hart? Great, so trust the guy who's been lying to us, but don't trust the woman who saved your life?"

"He trusts you," Chris countered.

"Then why didn't he tell me about his plan?"

"Because you'd try and talk him out of it," Willy said.

"I'd be right to do so, don't you agree?"

The three men avoided her gaze and didn't answer.

"What was he thinking?" Rose said, frustrated.

"That he needs to protect you," Willy said.

"By seeking out these violent men and risking his life?"

"Better his than yours," Michael said.

"But I'm not in danger."

"Apparently he thought you were," Willy said. "Plus, this way he'll be able to get the Feds what they need to charge the Russians."

"How will he do that?" Rose said.

"I'm guessing he'll record their conversation," Willy said.

"Or keep an open phone line so the Feds can record it," Chris offered.

"If they can even get reception up there." Rose shook her head. "It's dangerous and he's still recovering. This was a bad decision."

Rose walked away and went out front. She paced the porch, hands clasped together, saying a silent prayer.

Back in the kitchen, the guys were looking at her, probably blaming her for Noah's decision to "sacrifice" himself. Surely there had to be a better way to achieve the goal of protecting her.

Michael, clutching his ribs, stepped outside. "It's better if you stayed in the house with us."

"I'm frustrated. I need to process."

"I get it."

"Well, I don't get your friend. I really don't."

"Yeah, you do. If you think about it for a minute."

"I can't stand the thought that I could be the cause of his...his..."

"Don't say it. Noah's a clever guy. He might struggle with PTSD, but he can handle this. And he's got the Feds backing him up."

The door opened. Willy and Chris joined them, wearing serious expressions.

Rose gripped the porch banister and braced herself. "What?"

"The Feds lost contact," Willy said.

Which meant Noah was out there alone again, and once the Russians realized he had no intention of helping them...

No, she couldn't lose him like this. She'd be devastated. Oscar would be devastated.

"Oscar," she said softly. "Oscar can find him. Where is that dog anyway?"

She poked her head into the house. "Oscar, right here!"

Nothing. Then she had a horrible thought: What if he'd followed Noah into the mountains?

"Shh, listen," Chris said.

Muffled barking echoed across the property.

"Around back," Willy said.

They jogged to a supply shed on the edge of the property, the doors held shut by a thick branch. She pulled the branch free and opened the doors. Oscar dashed out, running and barking like crazy.

"What was he doing in there?" Chris said.

"Maybe he tried to follow Noah, so Noah locked him up for his own safety," Rose said. "Okay, you guys ready to find Noah?"

"Chris and I will find him," Willy said. "Michael and Rose, stay back and keep us updated about what's going on here."

"My dog, my search," Rose said.

"Noah wouldn't like—"

"Let's pack some supplies and go," she interrupted Willy, letting him know this was nonnegotiable. "We'll contact the Feds once we're en route."

Noah hiked the steep trail to the final rendezvous point. At first he wasn't sure why the Russians chose to meet in the wilderness to do business, but then he surmised they needed the isolation to stay off the Feds' radar, plus it would be an easy way to dispose of Noah's body.

He assumed they planned to kill him once they got what they wanted. He had a strategy for that, too.

Noah would do everything in his power to survive, but if he needed to sacrifice his life to end this threat against Rose…

…so be it.

At least Rose would be safe. If he died today, he would have given his life for something worthy—a remarkable woman he could have seen himself spending the rest of his life with.

He checked his phone. No reception. Another reason why the Russians picked this section of the national park. Noah couldn't call for help.

The Russians had changed the meetup location three times, this last change causing him to lose reception. Noah was unable to update Agent Hart about the new rendezvous point.

Noah was pretty sure he was alone out here.

Well, not totally alone. He allowed himself to feel God's presence, to embrace the strength of something he could not see with his own eyes.

Then another feeling pricked the back of his neck. Instinct told him to open the voice memo app on his phone.

A few minutes later, two men came around the corner and blocked the trail. They both carried rifles. Noah raised his hands in the air. A third, younger man joined them, holding up his phone.

"No signal," the younger man said. "We need reception to download the software."

"There's reception at the cabin," one of guys with a thick beard said. Noah assumed he was the leader.

"You brought the software?" the younger guy, probably the tech expert, asked Noah.

"No, but I've got the password to get us into the cloud to retrieve it."

"Give us the password," the tech said.

"What, and then you kill me? No, I'll type it in myself. I've set up a delay to give me time to disappear."

"How do we know it will work?" the bearded guy said.

"It'll work."

The tech guy and bearded leader exchanged looks. The leader motioned for Noah to continue up the trail.

They spoke perfect English, without a hint of an accent, which didn't surprise Noah. He'd heard about homegrown Russian agents, born and raised in the United States.

"I thought there'd be more of you," Noah said.

"Oh, there's more," the leader said.

"I want the same deal as Thomas," Noah said. "Two million dollars."

"You'll be lucky to get one million after all the trouble you and your friend caused us," the leader said.

Noah hoped the Feds were still tracking him, but he had to be realistic and consider they had probably lost him.

Yet Noah was recording the conversation, hoping someone could access it once this was over, even if Noah didn't survive.

They reached a turn and Noah spotted smoke drifting up from a cabin chimney in the distance. The end of the line.

Lord, if I don't make it... Take care of Rose.

"Once we get what we need, I'll hunt down G.I. Joe here, take him to the bridge and throw him off like he did to Victor," the third guy said.

"You'll never find me."

The guy gave him a smack in the back of the head that made Noah's eyes sting.

"Then I'll find your girlfriend and throw her off."

A chill raced down Noah's spine.

They were still going to kill Rose?

No, not if the Feds got here and arrested them. Noah had to stall, had to figure out a way to—

Barking echoed through the trees.

"Search-and-rescue," the younger guy said.

"Get him to the cabin," the bearded guy ordered.

The third man grabbed Noah's arm.

In the distance, Oscar burst out of the thick mass of trees, sprinting toward Noah.

"Easy target," the bearded guy muttered.

Aimed his gun.

"No!" Noah shoved him, causing him to miss the shot.

The bearded guy spun around and smacked

Noah in the side of the head with the gun. Noah went down.

"We need him conscious," the tech guy said.

Realizing the truth to his words, the leader lowered his gun and kicked Noah in the gut. Again, and again.

Then it abruptly stopped. Noah heard a grunt and a shot, then a second shot. He opened his eyes and saw the bearded guy on the ground with Willy on top of him. Willy winked at Noah as he tied the guy's hands behind his back.

Chris had disarmed the third guy and had him in a choke hold. The tech guy raised his hands in surrender.

"Feds are taking care of the Russians at the cabin," Willy said. "You okay?"

Noah nodded, struggling to catch his breath.

Oscar rushed up to Noah, and plopped down beside him with a whimper. Noah reached out and stroked his soft fur. "Good to see you, buddy."

Rose kneeled beside Noah and pressed her hand against his chest.

"You found me, again." Noah smiled and placed his hand over hers.

With an odd expression, she slowly withdrew her hand.

"It's okay, Rose. I'm okay," he said.

"I'm glad. But this is the last time, Noah. I can't do this anymore."

FIFTEEN

As Rose stood in the family's kitchen the next morning, she mused how the past week felt like a dream. Not a nightmare, because there were moments when Rose felt a strong sense of purpose and pride.

She'd even felt love.

At least what she thought was love. In the end, it was more of the same. Noah wanted to protect her, save her, because like everyone else, he saw her as a weak, fragile woman who couldn't take care of herself.

What she interpreted as love growing between them was actually duty, just like it had been with T.J.

Noah felt duty-bound to throw himself into the line of fire without conferring with her, asking her opinion.

"A quarter for your thoughts," her mom said, entering the kitchen.

"Wow, thanks." Rose kissed her on the cheek.

Mom went to pour coffee. "Why is Oscar pacing by the front window?"

"He needs a job."

"What about search-and-rescue?"

Rose shrugged. "Something tells me he'd be better suited for another line of work."

"But he found Noah."

"True, and comforted him. Which makes me wonder if he'd be a good emotional support dog."

"Well, all that pacing is driving me bonkers."

"Sorry. He misses his buddy." Rose couldn't even say Noah's name out loud. It hurt too much.

Mom joined Rose at the kitchen island. "Plans today?"

"A private training, group training and two house visits."

"Busy."

"Uh-huh."

"Then what are you still doing here?"

Rose shrugged.

"My sweet Rosie," her mom started.

"No lectures, okay?"

"No lecture, but may I share an observation?"

"Of course."

Mom leaned against the kitchen island. "You returned to the ranch a strong, independent woman, capable of dealing with any crisis, even the death of your sister." She sighed. "I don't think I realized what a grounding presence you've been. I've done a lot of reflection recently, and came to the conclusion that we've all been leaning on you because you are so remarkable, and able to hold us up. That's true strength, Rosie."

Strong. She called Rose strong, just like Noah had.

Mom took Rose's hand and nodded. "Yet I sense you're hiding out in my kitchen, avoiding something you need to deal with. Am I right?"

"Yeah, I guess."

"Well, stop. We all know that's not you. You're no coward, you can handle anything. Go on, get to it."

"Tough love, huh?"

"If it means helping you be your best self? Yes."

Rose hugged her mom, appreciating the compassion, and the challenge. Mom was right. Rose wasn't a coward and wouldn't hide out until Noah and his friends left Montana.

"Rosie, you'd better get out here!" her dad called from the front door.

She and Mom went to the porch where Dad was sitting with two dogs. Oscar followed and sniffed the dogs, all tails wagging.

"Who are these guys?" Rose asked, sitting on the porch. One of the dogs climbed into her lap. The tag read *Piper*.

"I found them secured to our fence at the end of the drive." Dad pulled a note out of his pocket and handed it to Rose.

"'This is Lucy and Piper,'" Rose read aloud. "'We can't keep them. We heard you are good with dogs. Please love them.'" Rose glanced at the midsize, mixed-breed dogs. "Huh."

"You could train them and put them up for adoption?" Dad said.

Piper looked at Rose with soulful golden eyes. "Or maybe train them to be emotional support dogs. The veterans at the Brewers' ranch would appreciate the company," Rose said. "In the meantime, I can't keep them at the apartment. Don't suppose I could move back in for a bit?" Rose smiled at her mom.

"Of course." Her mom winked. "We'll make a place for the pups in the barn. Go ahead and get your work done."

"Thanks." Rose stood and headed for her car. "Oscar, right here."

The dog trotted up beside her. "Might as well get this over with and say our goodbyes."

Noah still hadn't spoken to Rose. He heard she was okay, back to normal.

Normal? What did that even mean? He hadn't a clue.

As he, Willy and Chris watched Michael ride one of the horses around the pen at the Brewer Ranch, Noah appreciated how good it felt to be surrounded by friends, especially now.

He felt like he'd lost the two people who mattered most: Thomas to Russian agents and Rose to…

How did he lose her? He still wasn't sure, and she wasn't talking, hadn't communicated with him since they'd returned from the mountain the other day.

Noah wondered if she'd been in shock; she'd had her limit of violence and had shut down. She left the Brewer Ranch and essentially withdrew from his life. After everything they'd been through together, and how close they'd grown, it felt like he was walking around with a limb missing.

He didn't want to chase her, corner her or force the issue in any way because he knew her well enough to assume that would only make matters worse.

But he was desperate to know why she'd shut him out.

Willy had counseled Noah to give her space. Michael said she needed to process. Chris kept silent on the subject.

Yet the guys were not silent about their desire to stay in Montana permanently, maybe even buy the Brewer ranch and make it a veterans refuge. A worthy goal, one that would keep Noah close to Rose, geographically at least. They all had ideas about how to cover costs, maybe even by building rental cabins on the property and offering hiking adventures. It helped that three of them had professions that allowed them to work remotely in case they needed income. Mr. Brewer was excited about the prospect of the veterans buying his ranch when Willy spoke with him.

How would Rose feel about Noah being so close?

"You ready?" Willy said, snapping Noah out of his thoughts.

"Sure."

"Let's go, cowboy!" Chris called out to Michael.

Michael dismounted and passed the reins to Adam the wrangler.

The four men walked across the property and into the woods, hesitating at a spot with a panoramic view of the countryside.

"He'd like it here," Chris said.

Willy kneeled and dug into the earth, dropping seeds and covering them with dirt.

Then he pulled out Thomas's dog tags. Thomas had been wearing them when he was killed, and Agent Hart retrieved them for the guys. Thomas's body had been flown back to Virginia for a family burial, so this was their way of saying their goodbyes to their friend.

Michael shoved a thick stick into the earth and stepped back. Willy handed Noah the dog tags. He kneeled and draped them on the stick. "Friends for life and beyond."

"Friends for life and beyond," the others repeated.

The group hovered in silence for a few minutes, Noah embracing God's presence.

Then, the peaceful silence was broken by the sound of a barking dog.

"What is it with you and that dog?" Michael said.

The men chuckled, but Noah took a deep, calming breath. If Oscar was here that meant Rose had come, too.

Willy must have recognized trepidation on Noah's face, because he placed his hand on Noah's shoulder. "Speak your truth, brother. That's all you can do."

The guys headed back to the Brewer Ranch, Noah asking God for one more favor: to help him find the right words, because Noah honestly didn't know what to say to Rose to make things right.

As they approached the house, Noah spotted Beau walking toward him. His heart sank. Oscar must have come with Beau. Rose wasn't here after all.

"I thought I heard Oscar," Noah said.

"You did. Rose is here, too."

"Where?"

"The house."

Noah started for the house.

"Hang on. You might want to know what you're walking into first."

"Walking into?"

"I thought I was the only one who could make her that angry."

"Angry? What did I do? She wouldn't talk to me. Even to say goodbye."

"You need to listen to me for a minute." Beau blocked Noah's view of the house. "If you really want to know what's going on here."

Noah nodded that he did.

"You were the one person she thought believed in her, respected her. Our family, we love her, but we worry and tend to hover. She interprets that as we don't have faith in her."

"I have faith in her, I do. She's smart and strong. She's the most incredible woman I've ever known."

"Wow, you've got it bad for my little sister, huh?" He smiled.

Noah shrugged.

"Okay, then know this," Beau started. "The way she sees it, you made a plan without consulting her, which means you don't value her opinion."

"I saw photos of her in the Russians' account with instructions to find her. I lost it, man. All I could focus on was protecting her, no matter what the cost."

"I get that, I do. But another one of her hot buttons is being left out of the loop and treated like a child."

"This is different. You've got to know that."

"It doesn't matter what I think. You have to… I don't know, make her see your perspective? Or at the very least, apologize."

"Sure, of course. I can do that. I'll do whatever it takes to get her to talk to me again. I… I care about your sister. I guess that sounds stupid after only knowing her a week."

"Nah." Beau patted his shoulder. "I think she feels the same way. So, you've got that going for ya."

Noah glanced at the house. Hesitated.

"Be brave, soldier." Beau winked and walked away.

Noah started for the house, trying to figure out what to say to ease the tension between him and Rose. He tried to understand why she was so upset with him for wanting to protect her.

What was he missing? It didn't matter. He loved her and needed to fix this.

Please, God, open my heart to understanding.

It hit him then, how his decision to meet up with the Russians might have seemed disrespectful to Rose, especially after everything they'd been through. They'd shared intimate details of their lives; they were as close as any two people could possibly be in such a short period of time, yet he didn't share his plan to put his own life in danger to save hers.

Oscar suddenly burst through the front door and rushed up to Noah.

"Oscar!" Rose followed him out of the house and froze when she saw Noah.

He stroked the dog's head as Oscar sat on Noah's foot. "It's… It's good to see you, Rose," Noah said. "Everything go okay with the federal agents?"

"Sure, fine."

"I'm assuming you're glad this is all over."

"You have no idea."

She still wouldn't look at him.

"Rose, can we talk about why you're upset with me?"

She crossed her arms over her chest and narrowed her eyes at him.

"Please?" he said.

"Why does it even matter?"

"We're way past that. You know how much I care about you."

His comment seemed to rattle her.

"Just, just go, go back to Virginia," she said.

"Do you want me to go to Virginia?"

"No," she said, without hesitation. "Yes. I don't know."

"The guys and I like it here. We were thinking about pooling our resources and buying this place, maybe turn it into a guest ranch, or open it to struggling veterans. I can work remotely from anywhere, and so can Chris and Willy."

"Great, fine, whatever."

"Would it be okay with you if I stayed in Montana? I'd actually like to ask you out on a real date, something a little more low-key than running, hiding and dodging bullets."

She narrowed her eyes at him.

"You know, like grab pizza or go to the rodeo or something like that?"

"I can't be with a man who doesn't believe in me."

"I respect that, and I'm sorry if I triggered your trauma. When I thought the Russians were coming after you... Well, all I cared about, care about, is keeping you safe. I've fallen in love with you, Rose."

"Sorry, but that doesn't track."

"What do you mean?"

"'If you care about someone, you're honest. You trust them with your thoughts, and you include them in your decisions.' Your words, Noah."

He sighed. "You're right, but try to understand, I wasn't thinking clearly. I was terrified by the thought of you being hurt or... Rose, I messed up, but I'd like to spend the rest of my life making it up to you."

"Rest of...rest of your life? Whoa, I didn't see that coming."

"Sure you did." He took her hand and pulled her into a hug. Oscar danced around them, trying to get in on the action.

"You're smart, beautiful and kind," Noah said. "I'd be honored, and blessed, to have you in my life."

"You've become a very good communicator in the past week."

"I learned from the best."

And he kissed her.

From a ridge in the distance, a man peered through binoculars at the intimate moment unfolding between Noah and Rose. They looked so…

Happy. In love.

A grin eased across the man's lips. He sighed. All would be well. Contentment washed over him.

"You ready, T—"

"The name's Nick, remember? Nicholas Preston." The man lowered the binoculars and looked at the federal agent. "Yeah, let's go."

They climbed into a black Suburban and drove off.

* * * * *

Look for the next book in Hope White's Boulder Creek Ranch series, coming soon.

And in case you missed the first title in the series, you'll find Wilderness Hideout *wherever Love Inspired Suspense books are sold!*

Dear Reader,

Tracing a Fugitive was inspired by my love of the mountains and the wilderness, and how nature can calm the anguish that haunts us.

Trauma can leave a lasting wound on our emotional well-being. Through prayer and counsel we can lessen the burden, but for some it never really goes away. In some cases, we bury the trauma very deep, and in other cases we keep it within sight—both being strategies to protect ourselves from pain.

Noah Greene's trauma manifests as PTSD and is related to battle scars from having to carry out violent missions because of his devotion to our country. Rose's trauma is hidden away, yet still troubles her and impacts the way she sees the world. Together, and with faith in God, Noah and Rose are able to finally process their emotional scars and release the pressure that has held them back in life.

Their story illustrates how important it is to have faith in God and in the people we love, and to embrace the truth that lies within our hearts.

Peace,
Hope White

Get 4 FREE REWARDS!

We'll send you 2 FREE Books plus 2 FREE Mystery Gifts.

Both the **Love Inspired®** and **Love Inspired® Suspense** series feature compelling novels filled with inspirational romance, faith, forgiveness, and hope.

YES! Please send me 2 FREE novels from the Love Inspired or Love Inspired Suspense series and my 2 FREE gifts (gifts are worth about $10 retail). After receiving them, if I don't wish to receive any more books, I can return the shipping statement marked "cancel." If I don't cancel, I will receive 6 brand-new Love Inspired Larger-Print books or Love Inspired Suspense Larger-Print books every month and be billed just $5.99 each in the U.S. or $6.24 each in Canada. That is a savings of at least 17% off the cover price. It's quite a bargain! Shipping and handling is just 50¢ per book in the U.S. and $1.25 per book in Canada.* I understand that accepting the 2 free books and gifts places me under no obligation to buy anything. I can always return a shipment and cancel at any time. The free books and gifts are mine to keep no matter what I decide.

Choose one: ☐ **Love Inspired**
Larger-Print
(122/322 IDN GNWC)

☐ **Love Inspired Suspense**
Larger-Print
(107/307 IDN GNWN)

Name (please print)

Address   Apt. #

City   State/Province   Zip/Postal Code

Email: Please check this box ☐ if you would like to receive newsletters and promotional emails from Harlequin Enterprises ULC and its affiliates. You can unsubscribe anytime.

Mail to the **Harlequin Reader Service:**
IN U.S.A.: P.O. Box 1341, Buffalo, NY 14240-8531
IN CANADA: P.O. Box 603, Fort Erie, Ontario L2A 5X3

Want to try 2 free books from another series? Call 1-800-873-8635 or visit www.ReaderService.com.

LIRLIS22

COUNTRY LEGACY COLLECTION

19 FREE BOOKS IN ALL!

Cowboys, adventure and romance await you in this new collection! Enjoy superb reading all year long with books by bestselling authors like Diana Palmer, Sasha Summers and Marie Ferrarella!

YES! Please send me the **Country Legacy Collection!** This collection begins with 3 FREE books and 2 FREE gifts in the first shipment. Along with my 3 free books, I'll also get 3 more books from the **Country Legacy Collection**, which I may either return and owe nothing or keep for the low price of $24.60 U.S./$28.12 CDN each plus $2.99 U.S./$7.49 CDN for shipping and handling per shipment*. If I decide to continue, about once a month for 8 months, I will get 6 or 7 more books but will only pay for 4. That means 2 or 3 books in every shipment will be FREE! If I decide to keep the entire collection, I'll have paid for only 32 books because 19 are FREE! I understand that accepting the 3 free books and gifts places me under no obligation to buy anything. I can always return a shipment and cancel at any time. My free books and gifts are mine to keep no matter what I decide.

☐ 275 HCK 1939   ☐ 475 HCK 1939

Name (please print)

Address   Apt. #

City   State/Province   Zip/Postal Code

Mail to the Harlequin Reader Service:
IN U.S.A.: P.O. Box 1341, Buffalo, NY 14240-8571
IN CANADA: P.O. Box 603, Fort Erie, Ontario L2A 5X3

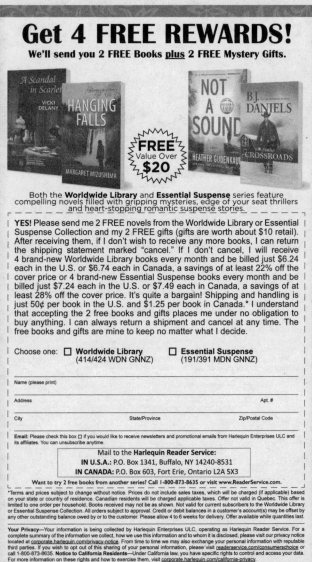